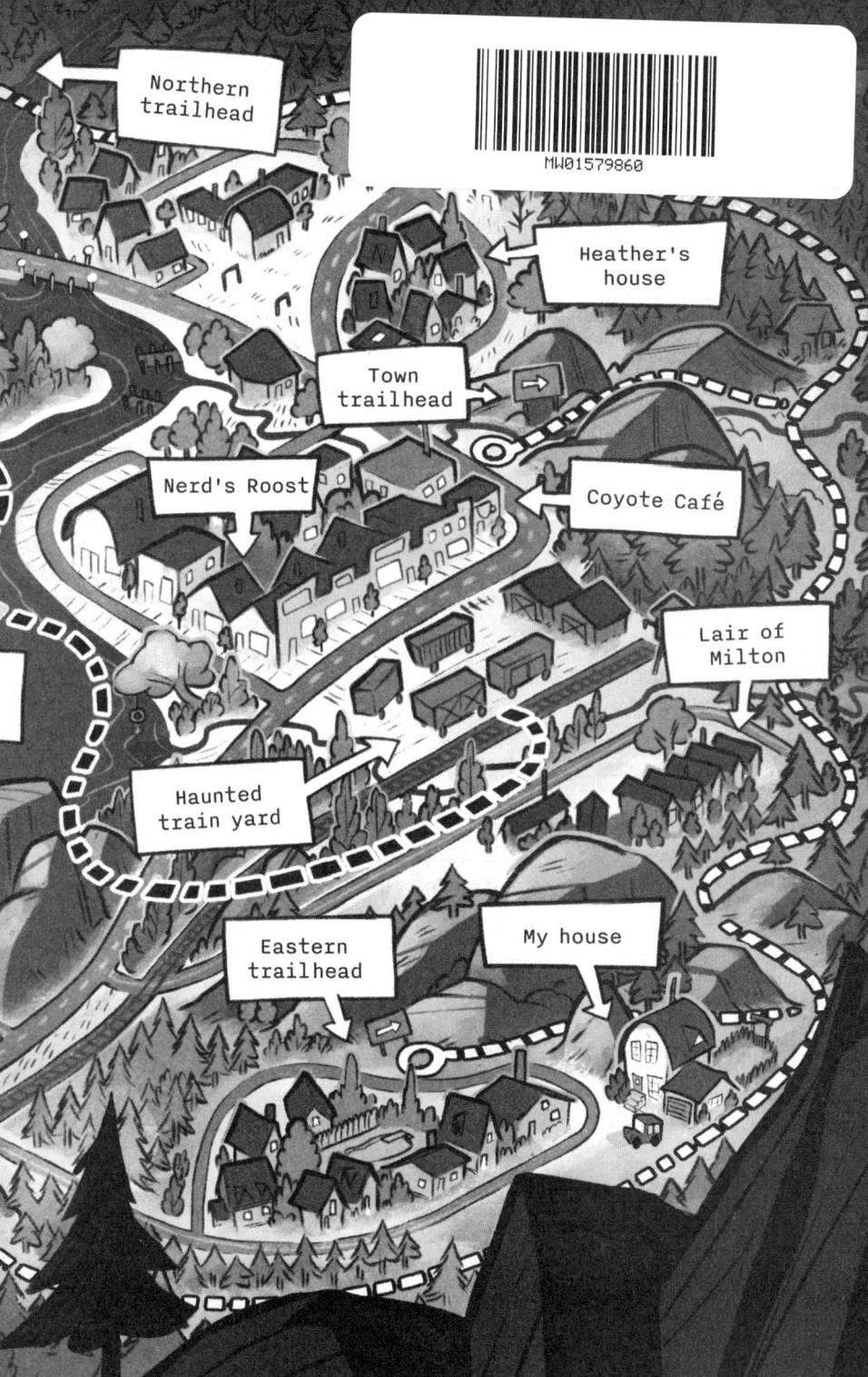

Thank you to my family and friends who watched all those weird scary movies with me at an age when it probably wasn't in any way appropriate. It had a lasting effect. —B.H.

© 2024 Braden Hallett (text and illustrations)

Cover art by Braden Hallett
Cover design by Braden Hallett, Sam Tse, and Rachel Nam
Interior designed by Braden Hallett, Sam Tse, and Rachel Nam

Edited by Claire Caldwell
Copyedited by Eleanor Gasparik
Proofread by Mary Ann Blair

We thank Natalie Carruthers for her contributions to this work.

Annick Press Ltd.
All rights reserved. No part of this work covered by the copyrights hereon may be reproduced or used in any form or by any means—graphic, electronic, or mechanical—without the prior written permission of the publisher.

This book is funded in part by the Government of Canada. *Ce livre est financé en partie par le gouvernement du Canada.* We acknowledge the support of the Canada Council for the Arts. *Nous remercions le Conseil des arts du Canada de son soutien.* We would like to acknowledge the funding support of the Ontario Arts Council (OAC) and the Government of Ontario for their support. We also acknowledge the support of the Government of Ontario through the Ontario Book Publishing Tax Credit, and through Ontario Creates.

 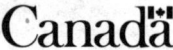

Library and Archives Canada Cataloguing in Publication

Title: Teddy vs. the slimy evil / written and illustrated by Braden Hallett.
Other titles: Teddy versus the slimy evil
Names: Hallett, Braden, author, illustrator.
Description: Series statement: Secrets of Ravensbarrow
Identifiers: Canadiana (print) 20240310896 | Canadiana (ebook) 2024031090X | ISBN 9781773219134 (hardcover) | ISBN 9781773219141 (softcover) | ISBN 9781773219158 (EPUB) | ISBN 9781773219165 (PDF)
Subjects: LCGFT: Novels. | LCGFT: Illustrated works.
Classification: LCC PS8615.A392458 T46 2024 | DDC jC813/.6—dc23

Published in the U.S.A. by Annick Press (U.S.) Ltd.
Distributed in Canada by University of Toronto Press.
Distributed in the U.S.A. by Publishers Group West.

Printed in Canada

annickpress.com
bradenhallett.com

Also available as an e-book. Please visit annickpress.com/ebooks for more details.

Secrets of Ravensbarrow
Teddy vs. the Slimy Evil

Braden Hallett

annick press
toronto · berkeley

Table of Contents

Chapter 1	Friday	1
Chapter 2	Mom. Dad. We Need to Talk.	8
Chapter 3	Bad News	17
Chapter 4	Cat-Flusher	25
Chapter 5	Yes, Martin Pembroke Is Actually My Cousin. Stop Asking. Ugh.	35
Chapter 6	Eager Help	45
Chapter 7	Ravensbarrow	51
Chapter 8	Shortcut	62
Chapter 9	Big Dog	74
Chapter 10	Martin and His Irritating Perfect Laugh	85
Chapter 11	Duggy Acts Weird	93
Chapter 12	Heather's Ghosts	102
Chapter 13	HAMSTERS!	109
Chapter 14	Duggy Acts REALLY Weird	116
Chapter 15	NOT DUGGY!	123
Chapter 16	The Worm	130
Chapter 17	Mr. Bear	141

Chapter 18	Fort Duggy	144
Chapter 19	The Den	151
Chapter 20	DUGGY!	159
Chapter 21	I Mess Up	164
Chapter 22	STUPID AUTOMATIC FLASH!	171
Chapter 23	Nerd's Roost	176
Chapter 24	Unexpected Help	183
Chapter 25	Milton	194
Chapter 26	Unmarked Trails	198
Chapter 27	Forgiveness (Kinda)	203
Chapter 28	The Ghost Bridge	208
Chapter 29	Ravensbarrow?	217
Chapter 30	So Many Squirrels!	223
Chapter 31	The Marble	232
Chapter 32	SCRAAAW!	241
Chapter 33	I Get a Terrible Idea	251
Chapter 34	BIG DOG!	260
Chapter 35	Board Games	273
Chapter 36	Home	284

Friday

Hi. I'm Teddy. I'm still an anxious kid.

Anxious

Super anxious

Anxiety meter off the charts

Anxiooooooooous

Why, you ask? Well, I'd just moved to a new house. In a new town. With a new school. New teachers. New friends. Also, I'm just ALWAYS ANXIOUS ANYWAYS!

We'd also survived an invasion of brain-eating hamsters.

That too.

And while we'd beaten the hamsters, they were still out there somewhere. Probably plotting. Planning. Sharpening their nasty little claws! I wasn't safe, and neither were Mom and Dad.

Don't forget about our cat!

Including Mr. Fuzzikins, yes!

Meow.

This is me, too

Brainivore Hamster

This place wasn't safe, and the only good idea I had was to move back home to Kamloops.

Easier said than done, Teddy!

So while I sat in the Ravensbee common area and tried to play cards with my friend Duggy, I was a little preoccupied.

Duggy clutched his last two cards and bumped up and down on his seat. He was the kind of kid who's always moving. He fidgeted, scratched, and kicked his feet.

"Umm..." I picked a card out of my hand at random and slammed it down on the table. "I cast..."—I looked down at the card I'd picked—"Gimbleward's thicket of locusty doom!"

Duggy heaved a huge sigh and pointed at the numbers on the top of the card I'd just played. "You can't play Gimbleward's thicket of locusty doom, Teddy! It costs five magi-beads. You only have four."

"Oh."

"Do you need me to explain the rules again?" Duggy reached into his backpack and pulled out the inch-thick manual for Card Combat II (featuring new spells such as Monfosilod's Carnivorous Kitty Carnage).

"No!" I said a little too quickly. "No, it's okay, Duggy. Thanks. I'm just a little worried."

"About what?" he asked.

Friends are for confiding in, right? "I'm still worried

about the whole hamster thing."

Duggy blushed and put his cards down on the table. "I'm really sorry about that, Teddy. What I did was pretty awful." Duggy had made a deal with the evil hamsters to save our lives. The catch was he was going to trade the lives of other kids to do it.

"No, I don't mean that," I said. Duggy looked relieved. He was still surprised that I'd forgiven him. I liked Duggy. He knew what it was like to be an outcast, which I used to be at my old school.

"I mean . . . How do we know that the hamsters aren't coming back?" I continued.

"What do you mean?"

I leaned in and whispered to keep the other kids in the common room from hearing me. "What if they're out there plotting their revenge? Sharpening their claws? Salivating at the thought of eating our brains?"

"Oh . . ." Duggy grinned uncertainly and shrugged. "I don't think you have to worry about that, Teddy. I haven't seen a single whisker. I don't think they're coming back."

"Okay . . ." I wasn't convinced.

Duggy twisted the cards in his hand and wiggled nervously. "Have you talked to Shane and Tienna about it?"

"No. We haven't had much time to talk." I started putting the cards away. Lunch was almost over. "Their class has been really busy this week. And besides, I've been trying to talk to them about you."

Duggy squirmed in his seat and looked at the ground. "What did they say?"

"Shane says you can hang out with us in the mornings." Shane was still a bit suspicious of Duggy, but at least he was logical about things.

"REALLY?!" Duggy exploded out of his seat. "What about Tienna?"

Teddy, if Duggy EVER dares show his face around me again, I will DESTROY him.

I shrugged. "I'm working on her. You can hang out until she gets to school."

"I just wish I could show her how sorry I am." Duggy shifted his backpack around.

"Don't worry, Duggy. She'll forgive you." I mean, Tienna couldn't stay angry FOREVER, could she?

Duggy smiled. "Thanks, Teddy." His eyes went wide as a thought hit him. "Ooh! Teddy! What are you doing this weekend?!"

"Unpacking. Family stuff."

"Well, if you have any time, you should come over to my house. In the backyard I'm building a FORT." Duggy stretched his arms out. "It's HUGE! It's got walls, and a roof, and I think I've found a TUNNEL under it!"

Building a fort in a muddy forest in the pouring rain. Fun.

"I'll see what I can do, Duggy." I wasn't REALLY lying; it's just that I had other priorities this weekend. I was going to stay warm and dry (and snuggle my cat) and convince my parents to move back to Kamloops. Hopefully.

Mom. Dad. We Need to Talk.

Okay, Teddy. You can do this.

They're gonna think we're making it up.

They'll believe me.

No they won't.

They're my parents. They HAVE to believe me.

Would YOU believe us?

Deep breath, Teddy.

I petted Mr. Fuzzikins one last time then heaved myself off the couch. "Hey Mom?"

Mom poked her head around the corner from the kitchen and wiped the sweat off her brow. She'd been busy organizing the kitchen all morning.

"What's up, Tedders? Finally ready to help? You could unpack your room."

I'd told Mom and Dad that it had been a rough week at school (which was true!) and they'd let me sit in front of the TV all morning. Since the only channel that worked in Ravensbarrow was public broadcast and the Internet wasn't hooked up yet, I'd spent the entire morning reading comic books instead. After reading every single one I owned, I'd finally worked up the nerve to talk about what happened at school.

"No, I don't want to unpack yet. I . . ."—I took a

deep breath—"I want to go home. I want to go back to Kamloops."

Mom stood silently for a moment. She motioned to the kitchen table. "Have a seat, Teddy." She leaned out the back door and called into the torrential rain. "Eddy, can you come inside for a minute?"

Oh wow! Family meeting time! Mom was taking this seriously.

A moment later my dad was in the kitchen dripping water and kicking off his boots. He'd been outside filling gopher holes. Every morning on the way to the car I stepped in one and twisted my ankle.

"That is one industrious gopher! I keep finding new holes." Dad shook the rain off his hat. "What's up?"

Mom looked over at me. "Teddy? Please continue."

I want to go home to Kamloops.

Dad looked worried. He leaned on the table. "Is this because of something that happened at school?"

"Well, yeah..."

"Is it bullies?" Dad turned to Mom. "I told you this would be a rougher school."

"No, Dad, it's not—"

"If you're being bullied, you need to tell us, Tedders." Mom put her hand on my arm. "I wish we'd gotten involved a lot sooner at your old school."

"Mom, it's not bullies!"

"Then what is it?" Dad looked confused. "Do you not like your teacher?"

"No, I—"

"Mr. Spinnaker seems nice!" Mom leaned back in her chair, as if nothing could possibly make me want to move back to Kamloops.

"It's not anybody at the school, it's just... This place is dangerous!"

"Dangerous how?" Dad demanded. "Is there someone dangerous at your school?"

"No, not someone!" I loved my parents, but sometimes they tried to put the puzzle together without all the pieces! "*Ravensbarrow* is dangerous."

"Teddy, I grew up here." Mom smirked. "The only remotely dangerous things in this town are bears and coyotes."

"Coyotes?" Dad looked over at Mom.

"Don't worry about it," she said.

They don't believe you, Teddy!

"Just . . . just listen to me!" I pleaded.

"We're listening, Teddy, but you need to tell us what's happening." Dad put on his calm-and-collected father tone. He only did that when he thought I was being childish.

You're stuck here, Teddy!

"I'm trying!" I gripped the sides of my chair.

"Okay, so why do you think it's dangerous here?" Mom asked.

"It . . . it's dangerous because . . ."

Rain pelted the window outside. Mom began to laugh.

My cheeks flushed. Mom KEPT laughing.

"Mom, don't LAUGH at me."

Mom wiped her tears away. She went to say something then burst into giggles again.

"Nice try, Teddy." Dad smiled and patted me on the shoulder. "But Ravensbarrow is our home now." He stood up and jammed his feet back into his muddy boots.

"Dad, you don't get it." I followed him to the back door. "Please, I'm telling the truth!"

Dad knelt down and hugged me. I pushed him away. "I don't want a hug! I want you to listen to me!"

"Teddy, you know why we moved here, right?"

"Well, yeah . . . You got a new job."

"It's a GOOD job, Teddy." Dad used his quiet and calm voice. It's not fair when he uses that voice. I wanted to be angry!

"I know, Dad." I started to calm down. Darn hypnotic dad voice!

"Ravensbarrow is our home, Teddy." Dad buttoned up his coat. "We're here to stay for a while."

"Okay..."

"Also, you told me about the brain-eating hamsters already." Dad winked. "From what I heard you can handle them if they come back."

Oh yeah. I guess I had told Dad already.

"I know it's not easy starting fresh, Teddy. But we're all here for you." Dad chuckled. "Now if a horde of brain-eating hamsters knocks down the door, I promise we'll drive away and never look back." He thought he was joking. But he was right.

I needed to find a hamster.

Bad News

I sat on the couch (surrounded by boxes) and hugged Mr. Fuzzikins. Mom laughed in the kitchen as she chatted on the phone. I got the feeling she was still laughing about me. Mr. Fuzzikins purred and snuggled closer. At least HE didn't laugh at me.

I stared at the blank TV and my stack of comics.

I needed that evidence, and I couldn't wait around for a hamster to just show up.

I had to go looking for it.

Dishes clanked and drawers rattled open and closed. Mom's laughter was now a chuckle. After a moment she sidled into the living room toward me. She had a plate with a white-cheese sandwich on it. (Cheese is fine. Milk is evil. Weird, I know.) She also held a can of pop.

We never get pop. Something must be wrong!

"Apology treat required?" Mom asked.

I stuck one hand out and hugged Mr. Fuzzikins with the other. I kept staring at the blank TV.

Mom put the can of pop in my hand and plonked the sandwich onto a stack of boxes beside the couch. She sat down, and the sudden weight slid me toward her. Our hips bumped. I didn't look at her.

"It's just that when you got all worked up there you sounded EXACTLY like your grandpa."

I stopped slurping. "Grandpa Theo?" I only had fuzzy memories of Grandpa Theo. I was named after him, though.

"That's right. He used to tell us all kinds of tall tales, and when he'd get to the exciting bits, he'd sound exactly like you! Combined with the fact that you were yelling about brain-eating hamsters I just couldn't help but laugh."

I took a bite of the sandwich. Mmm. Cheese. "It's okay. I get it." I slurped the can of pop dry. Mmm. Sugar.

"Do you want another one?" Mom asked.

TWO cans of pop?!

"But I never get two."

"Teddy, you know why we moved here, right?" Mom reached into the front pocket of her hoodie then plonked another can down in front of me.

She'd had it ready to go!

Something IS wrong!

"Well, yeah. Dad got a new job."

"That's right." Mom smiled.

Oh gosh this IS gonna be bad news.

"Also, we have family here."

"I know," I said. My auntie Morgan and cousins Martin and Milton lived about ten minutes away.

Mom's building up to something.

Mom cracked the can of pop and handed it to me.

Building up to something really bad!

"They've had a tough time ever since Uncle Toby left. Then your little cousin Milton got very sick. Auntie Morgan's had a hard time keeping up, so you're going to be seeing a lot more of your cousins."

"Okay..." This wasn't bad news. I already knew all of this. Sure, Milton was a five-year-old terror, but Martin always kept him in check.

"So Martin and Milton are coming over?"

"Well, not exactly," Mom said.

Uh-oh.

"It's just Milton."

WHAT?!

AGH!

"He'll be staying with us pretty often. Overnight sometimes."

AGH!

"So I need you to step up and be a good older cousin. Milton really looks up to you."

The doorbell rang! **DING-DONG!**

"That's probably them now." Mom smiled apologetically. She got up to answer the door.

I hurled Mr. Fuzzikins toward the kitchen (Meow!) and dove over the couch to hide. Maybe if I was very, VERY quiet, Milton wouldn't come looking for me.

He'll find us, Teddy! HE ALWAYS DOES!

Mom opened the door . . .

A second later I heard someone pounding into the house like a puppy with concrete feet. A tiny figure with a massive teddy bear came ripping around the couch and careened into me like a soggy missile.

Cat-Flusher

Milton

Mr. Bear

Obsessed with bears

Tantrum in human form

Enemy of Mr. Fuzzikins

Milton hugged me like a wet dog, leaving a greasy, sopping patch of rain and goldfish crackers on my shirt and pants. His colossal teddy bear flopped around in his hand.

I hobbled out from behind the couch with Milton hanging off me like a monkey.

Where's your cat?

I wanna play with him!

Mr. Fuzzikins, sensing the approach of his natural enemy, had hidden somewhere deep in our box-strewn house. It had only taken one "bath" to teach Mr. Fuzzikins to stay the heck away from Milton.

Martin came in and smiled brightly. He'd gotten taller. Ugh. Martin was a year older than me and everything I wasn't.

Martin

Tall

Handsome

Sociable

Smart

Athletic

He thinks he's so smart and funny and he's always so sincere and nice and AGH!!!

I was just a little bit jealous of Martin.

"Hi, Teddy!"

"Hi, Martin," I muttered.

"Milly!" Auntie Morgan and Mom did a weird handshake involving many bumps, twists, and wiggling fingers. "Thanks so much for watching Milton today."

"It's no trouble at all, Morg." Mom chuckled as she looked down at the parasite still hugging me.

"Hi," I muttered, muffled by her jacket. Auntie Morgan was nice, but she was INTENSE.

"Okay, Milton. A deal's a deal." Auntie Morgan bent down and fiddled behind Milton's ears. "Now that we're here, you need to wear your hearing aids." Milton grimaced as she nestled two powder-blue crescents behind his ears. He'd never needed hearing aids before . . .

She looked up at my mom and in a business-like mom voice said, "We just picked these up last week, so it's been an adjustment. He has no idea how loud he is if he's not wearing them." She patted Milton on the head. "Also, they help you hear stuff, baby boo!"

"Mr. Bear hears just fine, and he tells me everything!" Milton huffed.

"Mr. Bear is stuffed." Martin chuckled and patted his little brother. "He can't hear a thing."

I pried Milton's arms off me and pointed in the direction of Mr. Fuzzikins's litter box. "Maybe Mr. Fuzzikins is over there, Milton." He dashed away, leaving a trail of wet boot prints.

"I'd love to talk, but I have a double shift at work." Auntie Morgan handed a little backpack to Mom. "Martin has a lot of errands to run today, but he'll be by later to pick up Milton."

Wonderful. An entire afternoon with my little cousin. *There goes any chance to find a hamster today!*

Martin smiled warmly and clapped me on the shoulder. Geez, he was strong. Ow. "Bye Teddy! Thanks so much!" *Ugh. So sincere.*

I gave a little wave. Mom walked outside to talk to Auntie Morgan as she and Martin made their way back to their car. I was stuck here. With Milton.

Rain pelted the windows. I heard Milton rummaging around near Mr. Fuzzikins's litter box. I was about to slink away and find a hiding spot of my own when there was a knock at the door. Maybe Martin had forgotten something. Maybe Duggy wanted to play at his fort? I swung it open.

"Hi Teddy!" My heart jumped. Standing in the rain,

dripping water, were my two friends Tienna and Shane. I was saved! SAVED!

Tienna was shocked. "Whoa, Teddy, I did NOT think you were a hugger."

"What's wrong?" Shane asked. He peered behind me. "It's not the hamsters again, is it?!"

"Worse," I whispered.

Tienna swore and looked around. "Worse? What could be worse?"

"My cousin."

My mom came over as Auntie Morgan and Martin drove off. "Teddy, you didn't tell me that you'd made friends at school."

Tienna gently detached me from the hug and patted me on the head. "We were planning on showing Teddy some trails today, ma'am."

"That's a great idea!" Mom smiled. "I loved walking the trails around here as a kid. But only if you can tell me the golden rule of the trail society."

A walk! Yes! I could leave Milton here!

YES!

Tienna and Shane responded to Mom in unison. "Never ever leave the marked trails."

"Fantastic!" Mom gave a little thumbs-up. "Alright, Teddy, you can go." Mom perked up as she was hit with an idea. "And you can take Milton with you!"

I scrambled to get my boots on. "Mom, please, no! Please, NO, Mom!"

Milton's bear toque bobbed up from behind the couch like a shark fin. He'd given up his search for my cat.

"Did you say outside? I like going outside!" Milton grinned his gap-toothed goblin smile. He wasn't wearing his hearing aids anymore.

"See? He likes going outside." Mom held up my jacket.

"But MOM!" I tugged on it. Mom kept a tight hold on the collar.

"Teddy, look at me." Mom pointed at her eyes. "If Milton is outside, he's away from your cat. He can either go with you, or he can stay here and play with Mr. Fuzzikins."

Ha! Mom would never find Mr. Fuzzikins. My fuzzy buddy was a master of stealth!

Truly a wonder of sneaking and hiding!

A paragon of kitties!

Dad poked his head into the front hall. Mr. Fuzzikins, muzzle covered in jam, squirmed in his arms. "Your fuzzy younger brother got onto the counter again, Teddy. We're gonna need to give him a bath."

"I LOVE kitty baths!"

Yes, Martin Pembroke Is Actually My Cousin. Stop Asking. Ugh.

It was wet.

It was cold.

It was muddy.

It was PEEING rain (though Shane assured me it was just drizzling).

I HATE the rain!

And I missed my cat.

The Ravensbarrow trails were a twisting labyrinth

of mucky paths. They kind of looked like icky worms slithering through the forest. Apparently the main trail wriggled its way all around town and past my back door. I was pretty sure that Mom and Dad would make me walk to school now that I knew this path was here. Ugh.

Milton grabbed my hand with his greasy paw.

I rolled my eyes. I knew better than to shake him off.

"So I saw Martin Pembroke in your driveway," Tienna said. "Are you two related?"

"Yes." I continued trudging along.

"Really?" she asked.

"Yes!"

"Like, genetically? Not, like, through marriage or something?"

"YES!" I shouted. "Martin Pembroke is my cousin! My real cousin! My flesh-and-blood cousin!"

"No offense, Teddy, but HOW?" Tienna laughed. "Martin is . . . I dunno, he's . . ."

Better?

"Cool?" Shane offered.

"Well, yeah," Tienna agreed. "And smart. And funny. And nice. Everyone likes Martin."

Milton had tucked Mr. Bear into his backpack so the stuffy's mouth was near his ear. Milton listened to his bear theatrically then perked up. "He's my brother!"

"What's the gremlin's name again?" Tienna asked.

"I'm Milton!" There was a pause every time Milton had to pretend to listen to his bear. Geez that was annoying.

"He's my cousin, too." Ugh. This was so embarrassing.

"Wait a minute, I recognize you." Shane pointed at Milton. "You're the kindergartner who let our class frog loose in the staffroom."

"He wanted to go on an adventure!" Milton crowed.

Tienna gave Milton a high five. "Heck yeah! They blamed me for that one. It was hilarious. Froggy's day out!" Shane laughed.

Wonderful. Even my irritating little cousin was more fun to be around than me.

"Anyways, Teddy," said Shane, "we thought we'd show you the trails and the town today. Give you a break from unpacking. Maybe get some hot chocolate."

Milton watched Shane's lips moving and listened to Mr. Bear. "I like hot chocolate!" he barked as he whipped my hand back and forth.

"We also wanted to talk about what happened at school." Tienna grabbed Milton's other hand and swung it, too.

"What happened at school?" Milton kicked his feet up and I lurched sideways at the sudden weight. Tienna didn't even flinch. "Did they finally catch Mr. Hoppy?"

"Well..." Shane trailed off. I didn't know how to explain the hamster invasion either.

"The school was taken over by brain-eating hamsters," Tienna stated.

"AND I MISSED IT?!"

Uh-oh! Incoming tantrum!

Oh geez. The tantrums of Milton were legendary. But after a moment of intense sulking, Milton perked up. "Squirrel!" He tore off along the main trail. "Come back, Mr. Squirrel!"

Phew. Distracted.

Tienna chuckled. "Stay on the main trail, gremlin!" She turned to me. "Seriously though, Teddy"—Tienna picked up a rock and threw it at a tree with a CRACK!—"have you seen any hamsters?"

"No. Have you guys?" Maybe catching a hamster would be easier than I thought.

"It's been all quiet at my house," Tienna continued.

Darn.

"I spent a whole afternoon hamster-proofing the barn just in case." Shane wiped the rain off his glasses. "But I haven't seen any."

Somehow the fact that the hamsters had just disappeared was so much worse.

They could be ANYWHERE!

"Maybe they're afraid of your cat," Shane offered.

"You have a cat?" Tienna asked.

"You saw him," I said. "My dad was holding him at my house."

"THAT was a cat?!" Tienna grimaced.

"You've never seen a cat before?"

"Not in person, no!"

Weird.

"There aren't a lot of cats in Ravensbarrow, Teddy," Shane cut in.

"Really?!" I was astounded. "But they're so awesome! They're warm, and fuzzy, and snuggly, and cute, and..."

Tienna rolled her eyes. "We get it. You like cats."

"Mr. Fuzzikins is my fuzzy buddy."

"Gross. If that was a cat, I don't blame them for staying away. If I were a hamster, the first thing I'd do is get rid of it."

 She's right, Teddy.

"Tienna, don't say stuff like that." Shane frowned. "I'm pretty sure that they're long gone, Teddy."

Those hamsters are gonna eat your cat and then come for you and your parents.

Tienna grinned. "I'd bide my time and hide out in the forest until everyone had forgotten about me."

I bit my nails.

"Then I'd set a baited trap!"

Oh my gosh, it was true! The hamsters were gonna eat my cat and then come for me and my parents! They'd sneak into the house in the middle of the night and then burrow their way into our skulls and devour our brains!

AGH!

"Tienna, this is obviously freaking him out. Stop it!" Shane insisted.

Tienna pulled at my arm, but her voice was softer. "Don't bite your nails, Teddy. It's gross. Shane's right. The hamsters were probably all eaten by coyotes. I'm sure your cat's safe."

But I knew... I KNEW that they were still out there. Mr. Fuzzikins wasn't safe. My family wasn't safe. We HAD to leave. And in order to do that, I had to show my parents evidence of what I already knew.

You know, wrangling hamsters would be a whole lot easier with Shane and Tienna's help.

But how was I going to tell my friends that I wanted to leave? To leave them?

They don't need to know, Teddy!

I guess not. Not yet.

Eager Help

"Hey guys..." Aw geez, what could I say here. "How would you feel about going looking for the hamsters?"

Rain pelted the forest. Shane broke the silence. "Why?"

Good question, Shane.

Make something up, Teddy!

"I mean, talking hamsters are pretty... weird. So you know... Um."

I hoped everyone didn't notice that I was stalling for time. WHY find the hamsters, Teddy?

How can we convince Shane? What does he like?

I dunno. Drawing? Being annoyingly logical and asking really good questions?

Sounds sciencey. Does Shane like science?

"For science?" I offered.

Shane considered this then nodded. "Good point. Something supernatural like a talking hamster would be an amazing find for the scientific community."

"REALLY, Teddy?" Tienna's eyes burned into mine. Her brown eyes almost looked red. "You want to go looking for something that wants to eat your brain?" I glanced off into the misty woods.

You're a terrible liar, but they're buying it, Teddy. Keep going! What does Tienna like?

Violence?

Violence!

"Um ... yeah." I huddled down into my sopping hoodie. "And maybe you could ... teach them a lesson? Make them regret invading the school? Smash 'em?"

"YES, Teddy!" Tienna grabbed me around the neck. "Absolutely. I'm in!"

"We could even look for other supernatural stuff!" Shane said.

Wait.

What?

"Like what?" I struggled to break out of Tienna's headlock.

"My grandma told me about ghost bridges in the woods that appear and disappear at random. People cross them, but when the bridge moves on, the people can never come back. Maybe it's not just a story."

"I've heard about those, too," said Tienna. "Also Mrs. Sergeant told me about an owl with human hands that strangles lost hikers. It lives near Rook Rock." Tienna shook me in what she thought was a friendly way. "We could look for it!"

"No thank you," I squeaked.

What have you gotten us into, Teddy?!

ME? What have YOU gotten us into!

"We can look for all kinds of stuff, Teddy," Shane said.

This was NOT the direction I thought this conversation would go!

But maybe this could be a good thing. Maybe I could show my parents ANYTHING that was scary. And even if we didn't find anything, hamsters would be sure to pop up along the way.

"We could look for ghosts!" Shane continued.

"Werewolves!" Tienna added.

"What's a lake shark?" Shane raised an eyebrow.

"It's the shark in the lake! I've seen it!" Milton grinned.

Shane shrugged. "I mean, I guess a lake shark would be pretty supernatural."

"I know about all kinds of stuff like that!" Milton hopped in place excitedly.

"You do?" I rolled my eyes. "You're five."

"What, Mr. Bear? Oh! Yeah I do!" Milton yelled. He ran along the path. "Follow me, Teddy!"

"We ARE close to the lake," said Tienna, grinning.

"And we were planning on going to town for hot chocolate anyways," added Shane.

I heaved a sigh. Wonderful. Milton ALWAYS gets what Milton wants.

"Teddy!" Milton came dashing back. "Mr. Bear says that you have to go faster." He turned on his heel and flopped his way toward town.

Tienna ran after him. "I'll race you, gremlin!"

Shane shrugged. "I guess we're going shark hunting, Teddy."

And so we went to the lake.

Ravensbarrow

Shane lounged on the railing of the small pier. Rain made the lake shimmer. "I know we're looking for supernatural stuff, but it's a freshwater lake. We're days from the ocean. There are NO sharks here."

I gazed into the calm, rain-rippled water. "I'm pretty sure Shane's right, Milton." I still didn't want to jump in, though. I mean, sharks can lurk anywhere.

Rivers. Public pools. The bathtub.

Especially the bathtub!

"There IS a shark here! A big one!" Milton dug into his backpack. "Mr. Bear says we need bait." He pulled out his sandwich and tossed it into the water below.

Bloop.

A flock of sullen ducks approached the sandwich, but no sharks appeared.

Milton fidgeted for maybe ten seconds and then tugged on my sleeve. "I'm hungry."

And so we went to Coyote Café.

Not only was Milton taking up my entire day and ruining my chances of trapping an evil hamster...

And stealing your friends.

Not only that, but now he was drinking my hard-earned money. I'd had to take out the garbage, like, twice to earn that money. TWICE!

Milton sat at the table, happily eating the whipped cream off a large hot chocolate. I was lucky I had cash in my pocket (well, USED to have cash in my pocket). The last thing I needed was Milton throwing a tantrum in the café.

Shane and Tienna had settled down with their own hot chocolates. Shane had bought mine.

"It's a welcome-to-town present, Teddy." Shane smiled.

I smiled back, feeling a little guilty. It was the first time a friend had bought me something, and it was pricey.

Milton listened intently to Mr. Bear and stared at our mouths like he was trying to read our lips.

"All right!" Tienna slugged back her molten cocoa like water and wiped her mouth on her forearm. "What kinds of creepy things are we looking for, since the lake shark was a bust?"

Milton's eyes widened as he held Mr. Bear to his ear. "Ooh! Ooh! I know! The lady who works here is a VAMPIRE!"

I scowled. Brain-eating hamsters? Sure. A vampire working a small café during the lunch rush? I just couldn't see it.

Milton burped. He'd eaten all the whipped cream but left the hot chocolate almost untouched. "I'm bored."

I rolled my eyes. "Milton, we just got here."

"And this place is too loud!" Milton crossed his arms defiantly.

"The comic shop's next door," Shane offered. "Lots of games and stuff."

Mr. Bear relayed the message. "I like games." Milton stood up and tugged on my arm. "Come on, Teddy!"

And so we poured our hot chocolate into paper cups and went to the Nerd's Roost.

The Nerd's Roost was actually really neat!

It was part comic shop, part gaming store, and part antique emporium. Large tables were set up so people could play from a huge selection of free games. Comics lined the shelves from floor to ceiling. The back room was crammed with more gaming tables and ancient antiques, all with little tags describing what they were and where they came from.

One good store doesn't make it a good home, Teddy.

I guess not . . .

Shane was digging through the stacks of board games. Tienna was following Milton around. She really seemed to like him. Ugh. She just didn't know him well enough yet. They made their way back toward me.

"All right, gremlin, so what's weird and supernatural about this place?" Tienna asked.

"What? Weird about this place? Ooh! Ooh! The owner is a time traveler!"

"Candice is NOT a time traveler," Tienna said as she tousled Milton's hair.

The woman behind the counter grinned. "I totally am," she said, snapping her round goggles into place. "These are my special tachyon goggles. They let me see back into my present time, which is your future, primitive humans."

"See!" Milton's eyes were wide. "Pat-ee-ons!"

GEEZ Milton was gullible. Time travel? REALLY?!

Shane walked up to us with a stack of board games teetering in his arms. "I'm a little more open-minded than I used to be, Candice, but time travel is impossible." I grabbed one of the boxes off the stack before it could fall over. "Thanks, Teddy."

"You have no creativity in your soul, Shane," Candice huffed. "It ruins your first marriage."

"How does she know that?" Milton said, amazed.

"She can see the future, Shane." Tienna grinned. "She can see your final days bent over a microscope, dying from a lack of imagination."

Shane stuck out his tongue. "Tell that to my sketchbook." Shane's doodles were creative. "ANYWAYS! I have a few options for us . . ."

"I like board games!" Milton said way too loudly. A few patrons' eyes widen at the sudden noise.

Tienna groaned. "Not more board games. They're boring."

"You might like Zombie Splat. You roll dice to kill zombies. Extra points for the bloodiest kill."

"I SUPPOSE I'll give it a try," Tienna said warily.

"But what about paranormal stuff?" I asked. "What about the hamsters? Creepy things? EVIL things?!"

"There's a pyramid of human skulls in the forest!" Milton piped up. "The squirrels made it."

Tienna chuckled. "This kid is awesome."

"Teddy, we're not going to find anything today," said Shane as he rattled dice in a cup. "And it's tough to do any investigation with your little cousin around. Now, what color do you want?"

"RED!" Milton shriek-giggled. Everyone in the store jumped. At least I wasn't the only one annoyed by Milton.

"But . . . but I was REALLY hoping to find a hamster or . . . or something today." I wanted to go home! NOW!

Shane peered over the top of the rule book he was reading. "I'm willing to bet the hamsters are long gone. And we've got years to investigate the supernatural."

YEARS?!

"Let's talk about it at school," he said.

My plan lay in shambles.

We're stuck here, Teddy.

Stuck in this rainy, soggy town that I was certain was filled with vengeful (stealthy) hamsters . . .

Forever.

I got that anxious feeling in the pit of my stomach and moved my hand up to my mouth to bite my nails. Tienna grabbed my hand then smiled.

"Play some board games with us, Teddy."

And so we played board games until the dim daylight of rainy Ravensbarrow got dimmer and dimmer.

Zombie Splat was actually pretty fun.

Shortcut

There was no sunset in Ravensbarrow. The gray light of day faded until suddenly it was dark. I could still make out the shapes of the treetops against the dark iron sky, but pretty soon it would be pitch-black. We'd lost track of time, so Tienna and Shane had both had to run home. They'd pointed me in the right direction and told me I'd be fine. Just follow the main trail, Teddy.

I wasn't so sure.

As Milton and I trudged toward home, a thick fog crept onto the trail. The rain fell harder.

Doesn't it EVER stop raining here?!

"Oh no!" Milton cried. "Mr. Bear's gonna get wet!"

I rolled my eyes. "Milton, Mr. Bear is already wet. He's been wet all day." I turned to look at Milton.

Uh-oh.

I knew that face.

Incoming tantrum!

"I NEED Mr. Bear!" Milton sobbed. "He hears for me. Without him I'm gonna have to wear my hearing aids. I HATE them!"

"Will he fit in your backpack?" I looked up at the sky.

It's getting darker, Teddy.

"No. He's too big!"

Oh geez. Umm. Oh geez. What could I do here? I never had to deal with Milton when he got riled up. Mom and Martin always stepped in.

"What are we gonna do?!" Milton teared up then hugged me. Oh geez.

What would Martin do here?

I put on my best confident-older-cousin voice and spoke a little louder.

"Um. Okay, Milton, here's what we're gonna do."

You sound like a squeaky cowboy.

I leaned down and tried to smile. I'm pretty sure I looked like some demented sci-fi hyena with my braces out in the open.

"We're gonna run as fast as we can back to my house."

Milton sniffled.

"And then Mr. Bear will be just fine."

Milton nodded.

Hey, this good older-cousin thing wasn't too hard!

"The faster we get home, the drier Mr. Bear will be."

Milton smiled.

Hey, I was kinda good at this!

"Oh!" Milton shouted and perked up, shaking raindrops everywhere. "I know a shortcut!"

Uh-oh.

Milton took off like a shot away from the main trail.

Into the mist.

"Follow me, Teddy!"

"Wait! Milton! We can't go on any unmarked trails!" I could just make out Milton's bear-ears bouncing away from me.

Milton paused to listen to Mr. Bear. "It's not an unmarked trail!" Milton called. He sounded so far away.

"Milton! I can't keep up!" How was he so FAST?!

"It's through the haunted train yard..." Milton's little voice was a muffled echo.

I ran up to the railroad. Just beyond it, a cluttered train yard loomed out of the mist. I could barely make out a maze of crates, old train cars, and a tangle of rail tracks.

The rain fell harder . . .

The fog got thicker . . .

The last light faded . . .

And I couldn't see Milton.

Silence.

I stood on the side of the railroad and tore at my nails. I'd heard a few stories about kids playing around trains and none of them had ended well. Mom and Dad would never forgive me if they knew that I'd been messing around in a train yard.

But I couldn't leave Milton behind . . .

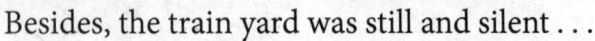
I'd be fine with it.

Oh shut up!

Besides, the train yard was still and silent...

What would Martin do?

I looked both ways then ran across the tracks and slid down the gravel slope on the other side.

My feet crunched on the gravel. Unused train cars sat on lengths of rail, forming the walls of a misty labyrinth. Everything smelled soggy.

"Milton!"

Silence.

And then...

Yip!

Yip?

The noise was punctuated by a high howl. I had heard this howl in Kamloops. Often. It was a coyote.

"Milton!"

"Go away, Mr. Coyote. I don't have any food for you today."

Oh my gosh! I ran toward Milton's voice and came

to a screeching halt. Milton was sternly lecturing a small coyote. It was a ragged, thin, scruffy thing with a snaggle-toothed grin. I grabbed Milton by the shoulders.

"Milton, we can't be here."

Another scruffy figure popped up beside Mr. Coyote.

"Go on!" Milton made shooing motions with his hands. Another two coyotes joined, making it official—we were facing a pack.

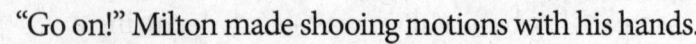

"Um . . ." Milton started to back away.

"It's . . . it's okay, Milton." I tried to put on my older-cousin voice, but all that came out was a squeak. "Coyotes don't attack people."

Coyotes don't attack ADULTS, Teddy.

Three more coyotes began to creep in from either side. Mr. Coyote grinned and licked his chops.

The coyotes leaped!

We bravely stood our ground.

No, Teddy. That's not what happened.

We carried out a tactical withdrawal?

No, Teddy. Tell the truth.

Okay... We ran, screaming, pursued by the coyotes. Honestly, it was probably the WORST thing we could have done, but when my lizard brain says "run," I RUN!

Big Dog

I had no idea where we were going. Milton ran. I followed.

We screeched around a corner, and I saw Mr. Bear wiggle free of his sling on Milton's back. With a wet florp, Mr. Bear flooped to the ground. Good! Something to distract the coyotes!

I glanced over my shoulder and saw Mr. Coyote and his friends tearing at Mr. Bear in triumph. Stuffing flew everywhere.

We could get away!

Mr. Bear! NOOOO!

Milton tore past me and charged the coyotes as they tore into Mr. Bear. "LET HIM GO! BAD, BAD POOP-FACE COYOTE!"

He tugged at Mr. Bear's legs. Mr. Coyote tugged at Mr. Bear's arms. The other coyotes yipped, yowled, and leaped around like they were betting on a wrestling match.

Oh gosh. What was I supposed to do here?! My feet were glued to the ground.

Run, Teddy!

I couldn't run! Milton would be eaten!

Fight, then, Teddy! Pick up a rock!

I looked at all the coyotes' sharp, snapping teeth. My feet didn't budge.

Do something, Teddy!

I tried. I really did. But all I did was let out a little squeak.

The other coyotes got closer to Milton. They licked their chops. Drool spilled from their mouths.

They were hungry.

Milton fell on his butt in the mud and Mr. Bear fell to the ground. I fell backward to the ground, too.

WHAT THE HECK WAS THAT!

Mr. Coyote hung from the dog's massive jaws and thrashed around, trying to free himself.

YIP! YIP YIP! YIPYIPYIP!

The dog glanced down at us with its glowing blue eyes. A growl like a rolling boulder rumbled in its throat.

YIPYIPYIP! YIP! YIPYIP!

A flash of lightning cracked, and as the thunder struck (KABOOM!), the dog tossed Mr. Coyote in the air and opened its jaws wide as a swimming pool.

YIIIIIIIIIIIIIIP!

CRUNCH

The dog chewed.

I looked away, but Milton watched with a horrified look on his little face.

I hoped he couldn't hear what I could . . .

The coyotes, being much smarter than Milton and me, ran for their lives.

The dog stayed. It sat there. Panting.

I couldn't move. My lizard brain was certain that if I dared to even twitch, the house-sized train yard dog would eat me in an instant.

Milton looked at Mr. Bear, lying on the ground at the dog's feet.

Milton looked at me. I shook my head. No, Milton! No, no, no!

The dog licked its chops, smacking its mattress-sized tongue against its lips.

Milton REALLY loved Mr. Bear.

I tried to say, "Milton, you irritating, puny, monumentally STUPID little monster!" But all that came out was a hoarse, quivering almost-silent "dog... big... dog..."

Milton crawled inch by inch. He picked up his stuffed friend, put him back in his backpack, and crept back toward me. The crunch of his rain boots on the gravel was drowned out by the torrential rain.

The dog sniffed the air.

Milton grinned as he crept up beside me. He tugged on my jacket. I kept hyperventilating and looked at my little cousin. I couldn't move.

Milton smiled reassuringly and put one hand on my shoulder and the other under my elbow.

Milton lifted. With his help I slowly got to my feet. I didn't take my eyes off the dog. It hadn't seen us. We could get away! I looked at Milton and tried to smile. He wasn't gonna leave me behind. He'd grown up a lot since the last time I'd seen him.

Milton thought that he was whispering.

Milton had left his hearing aids back at my house.

Milton was not whispering.

The dog spoke in a hoarse gravelly whisper. The hot stench of at least one dead coyote flowed over us.

The ogre-spaniel could talk!

AGH!

I'M SICK OF CHILDREN WANDERING THROUGH MY HOME.

STAY OUT OF MY TRAIN YARD! OR I'LL EAT YOU!

The ground shook as the hound's thunderous barking threatened to tear the train yard to pieces. Milton grabbed my hand and dragged me away as we screamed and ran out of the train yard into the dark misty night.

Martin and His Irritating Perfect Laugh

"Milton! Teddy!"

An arm like an iron bar caught me by my shoulder. It was Martin. I tried to keep running (we were still WAY too close to the train yard), but Martin held me in place.

"Martin!" Milton hugged Mr. Bear and shouted in terror, "Martin! Dog! Big dog! BIG!"

"BIG!" I agreed. "Big dog!" I turned and pointed wildly toward the train yard. "BIG!" I yelled. "BIG!"

"Oh man, you guys came through the train yard?" Martin shook his head and gave Milton a hug. "Yeah, the train company has a new guard dog. She's there to scare off the coyotes. Definitely a big dog."

"SCARE OFF?!" I waved my arms. "IT ATE ONE RIGHT IN FRONT OF US!"

"What?" Martin tried to corral Milton. "Snofur? Nah. She barks real loud and she's got really big teeth, but she's a softy."

"WHAT?!"

"BIG DOG!" Milton yelled. "BIG DOG, MARTIN!"

"I get it, Milton," Martin laughed. "Big dog. Now come on, let's go home." He grabbed Milton's hand as he continued thrashing around. "Do you wanna come to our house, Teddy? We can call your parents to come pick you up."

Why did he have to be so calm and collected all the time? Wasn't he listening?!

"You're not LISTENING, Martin!" Milton yelled, vibrating with rage.

"Geez you're jumpy!" Martin pulled Milton along the trail. "Sometimes dogs can seem really big when you're a little kid, okay?"

I took a deep breath and caught up to my cousins. My hands were still shaking. "Martin, seriously. It wasn't just a dog. It was the size of a house."

Martin laughed that irritating perfect laugh of his. "I mean, Snofur is a big dog, but you were just seeing things."

"No I wasn't!"

"What?" Milton listened intently to Mr. Bear. "No we weren't!" he agreed.

Geez I wish I had a picture of that dog. Wait a minute... Why didn't I bring a camera with me?! Dad has a camera! WE COULD'VE JUST ASKED! I'd gone looking for hamsters and I hadn't even thought to bring a camera—and then found a supernatural whale-sized ogre-spaniel that threatened to eat me alive!

Nice job, Teddy.

"No more cutting through the train yard, okay?" Martin said, gripping Milton's hand like a vice. "No more shortcuts." Milton had accepted his fate and trudged sullenly alongside his brother.

"Martin, we're not lying," I pleaded.

"Okay, okay." Martin sighed. "Look, maybe sometime this week you and I can go and see the dog, okay? We'll bring some cheese. If you give Snofur cheese, she'll be your best friend forever."

"Martin, we're not talking about the same dog!"

"All dogs love cheese, Teddy." Martin smiled knowingly.

Martin didn't get it. But Milton and I did.

Our shoes crunched along the gravel on the way to Martin and Milton's trailer. A sign that read "Happy Valley Trailer Park" loomed out of the mist and rain. The conversation turned from dogs to hearing aids.

"What do you mean, you don't know where your hearing aids are?" Martin looked as close as he ever got to angry, which was mildly irritated.

"I mean I don't know." Milton shrugged.

"I saw him take them out at my house," I offered.

Milton glared at me mutinously.

"Sorry," I said. I actually was kind of sorry. Milton REALLY hated those hearing aids.

"Thanks, Teddy." Martin clapped me on the shoulder. "Losing them would've been a disaster. Mom's having a really hard time as it is without having to buy new hearing aids. Can you bring them with you to school tomorrow?"

"Sure."

Martin opened his front door and turned on the lights.

He sighed. The trailer was a total mess.

Milton ran inside. "Mommy! We're home!"

Martin took a pile of laundry off one of the chairs. "Mom's working late, Milton."

"Aww." Milton's smile crashed. "She's always working."

"I know, bud. If you get into your pajamas we can play some video games before bed, though!"

"Yay!" Milton scooted off.

For just a second, Martin looked tired and anxious. But then his normal smile took over. "Have a seat, Teddy." He patted the chair he'd just cleared. "I'm sorry about the clutter."

I sat down. Martin handed me a phone to call my parents then started folding laundry. There was a cord attaching the phone to the wall. Weird. Dad picked up and said he'd be over in a few minutes.

"Can I get you anything, Teddy?" Martin kept folding. "I think we have some ice cream in the freezer."

"What? No thanks," I said. "Dad'll be here in a second."

Milton burst out of his room dressed in bear jammies. "VIDEO GAMES!" He tugged on Martin's sleeve. "Come play, Martin!"

Martin put down Milton's undies that he was folding. "Sure, Milton, but just for a bit." He let himself be led over to the couch. "I still have to make our lunches for tomorrow."

I took another look around. A few bags of groceries

and several bottles of medicine were strewn across the counter.

"Martin?" The last time we'd visited Auntie Morgan and the cousins their home had been clean. Not, like, spotless, but definitely not this messy. Something had changed. "Is everything okay?"

Martin looked worried for a second, but then the smile came back. "Everything's fine, Teddy."

Wheels crunched on the gravel outside. "My dad's here." I got my hat and shoes back on.

Martin got up and gave me a hug then clapped me on the shoulders. "I'll see you tomorrow at school, Teddy."

"Yeah."

I was silent on the drive home. As we pulled into our driveway, Dad heaved a sigh.

"Thank you, Teddy, for watching your cousin today."

"It's okay." I thought for a moment. "There's a lot going on in their lives, isn't there, Dad?"

"There is," he said, nodding. "So what did you get up to?"

"We were almost eaten by a dog the size of a barn."

"Neat!"

Dad still didn't get it. But at least I knew I was right. We had to get out of Ravensbarrow. And now I had another way to get my proof.

Duggy Acts Weird

"It's true!" Milton chipped in as Mr. Bear nodded. He had run up to me in the schoolyard that morning and followed me inside. He insisted that I needed someone to watch out for me since I was new in town.

Heather put her hand to her chest and loudly proclaimed, "Well, I believe you, Teddy."

"You agree with EVERYTHING Teddy says." Shane rolled his eyes. "It was just a big mean dog. Ravensbarrow has tons of big mean dogs."

I whispered in Shane's ear, "brain-eating hamsters, Shane." We hadn't told Heather (formerly Hamster-Girl) about her hamster's part in the whole "eat everyone's brains" thing last week.

"Okay, okay, I believe you," Shane grumbled. "But you can't blame me for being skeptical. When I think of the supernatural, I think of things like werewolves, not really big dogs. And there ARE a lot of dogs around here."

"Well, it was way scarier than a werewolf, and next time I'll be ready." I pulled Dad's old phone out of my pocket.

Shane smirked. "You know there's no reception in

Ravensbarrow, right, Teddy? That won't work here."

Yet ANOTHER reason to leave, Teddy.

I shrugged. "It doesn't matter. I don't need the phone. I just need the camera."

"Why?" Heather asked. "And what's this about werewolves?"

"They're lookin' for soo-per-nach-ral things!" Milton shouted, eager to be part of the conversation. I'd tried to give him back his hearing aids, but he'd refused. He kept saying Mr. Bear could hear for him. Milton even wiggled Mr. Bear's head as if he were whispering. It was almost convincing.

I turned to Heather. "Haunted... how?" I'd seen shows about the most-haunted places in Canada. They involved a lot of people stumbling about asking if there were any ghosts around. I needed concrete proof.

Heather looked a little embarrassed. "Well... you guys probably won't believe me."

"You might be surprised," Shane said.

"Furniture moves on its own, and I hear voices from nowhere."

It might not be enough to prove to my parents that this place was dangerous (not like that bloodthirsty dog), but it would be a start!

"Come over after school. The ghosts are a little shy around my parents, but they won't be home until dinner."

"Oh, there's Duggy!" I waved at him. "Maybe he'll wanna come along."

"Not if Tienna has anything to say about it," Shane said.

"She's not here. She doesn't get a vote." I glanced around. "Keep an eye out for her, though, okay?"

I waved again. "Duggy! Over here!"

Duggy put on an exaggerated grin and strolled over. "Hello friends!"

Shane and I gave each other a look. Duggy did not stroll. Duggy was normally a chipmunk. Right now he was acting like a . . . a . . .

Capybara?

Sure. A capybara.

Heather gave Duggy a withering look. She was far too polite to say anything, but Duggy smelled today. He smelled a lot. He smelled . . . cheesy.

Duggy wasn't the cleanest kid around, but he'd never smelled cheesy before.

Goofy smile?

Cheesy?

"Is everything okay, Duggy?" I asked.

"Everything is fine, friend. Why do you ask?"

"Well . . ." I had no idea what my lines were here. How do you tell someone they smell like cheese?"

"You stink!" Milton shouted.

"Milton!" Martin strode toward us with a disappointed older-brother look on his face. "That was very rude."

"But he does!" Milton pointed at Duggy.

"Milton, you can't just—" Martin raised his eyebrows as he got closer. "Oof. Duggy, I'm really sorry, but you may need to change your clothes or something."

Duggy grinned. "No, I am sorry. They are dirty clothes. Tomorrow I will wear clean ones."

"Teddy, did you remember the hearing aids?" Martin asked.

"Yeah." I dug through my backpack. "They were in Mr. Fuzzikins's litter box."

Martin shook his head. Milton looked back with a defiant frown.

"We cleaned them," I said, handing them over.

"Okay, buddy." Martin sighed and moved toward his little brother. "I know you don't like these things."

"No! I don't!" Milton hugged Mr. Bear and backed away.

Martin took Milton aside. He launched into a conversation I could tell they'd had more than once. Milton pouted but nodded sullenly from time to time. I turned back to Shane and Duggy.

"So, Teh-dee, my friend," Duggy said, "what conversation was taking place before I arrived?"

Shane, Heather, and I shared another look.

Shane shrugged and opened his sketchbook back up. "Teddy was telling us about a dog the size of a house that lives in the train yard."

"I was unaware of terrestrial mega-fauna in this area. How fascinating!"

We all stared at Duggy, speechless.

Martin's voice broke the awkward silence. "Okay, Milton. Deal. You only have to wear them at school this week." Milton nodded then slipped in one of his hearing aids.

Milton sprinted wildly down the hall, bounced off a locker, and then ducked into the boys' bathroom. Martin ran after him.

"Milton! Milton, what's wrong?!"

"Interesting." Duggy narrowed his eyes and watched as Martin followed Milton into the bathroom. "Very interesting."

Interesting?! What the heck, Duggy?

That wasn't interesting. I knew that scream. I made that scream a lot last week during the hamster invasion.

Milton was terrified.

Heather's Ghosts

Tienna, Shane, Heather, and I walked along the crooked sidewalk toward Heather's house. Milton had been so riled up that Martin had taken him home early. Geez I hoped he was okay. I hadn't seen Duggy the rest of the day, either.

"Aw, man, I can't believe I missed it," Tienna snarled. "And the dog said it was gonna eat you?"

"Yeah," I said. "Just like it ate the coyote."

"I am VERY disappointed," Tienna huffed.

"That it didn't eat Teddy?" Shane raised an eyebrow.

"I mean . . . that might have been cool to see, too!"

"Tienna!" Heather turned around and glared at her. "Don't joke about something so awful." She dug through her backpack for her house keys.

"Aw, Teddy knows I'm kidding." Tienna put an arm around my shoulders.

"Your special brand of friendship is hard to miss, yes."

Shane rolled his eyes. Tienna grinned and punched his arm.

These really were my friends. And here I was looking for evidence of the supernatural so I could go home. So I could ditch them. ABANDON them!

Hey! Focus, Teddy! We wanna go HOME!

I guess. You're right. We can't stay in this place.

Heather opened the front door to her house.

Heather put her finger to her lips and motioned us to follow her. We crept up the stairs. As we got near the top, I heard whispering voices. A chorus of whispering. We peeked over the top stair and saw an empty hallway. If Heather's house had ghosts, there were a lot of them!

"Hello?" Heather called out. The voices stopped instantly. "See?!" she said, smiling.

"Okay, that IS weird," Shane agreed.

Oh my gosh! Ghosts! I got my camera ready.

"Okay, now look in my room." Heather beckoned us along the hall to a door covered in hamster stickers.

We glanced around Heather's room. It was spotless. Hamster posters covered every bit of her walls, and hamster stuffies were piled neatly in one corner. Hamster books crowded the many bookshelves. Her bed (perfectly made up with hamster-patterned sheets) sat under a window. A desk and simple wooden chair were placed beside it. On a small table a cage gleamed. A single occupant snuffled about and squeaked. Scrabbles.

Heather closed the door, leaving us in the hallway,

and then in a loud voice proclaimed, "Boy, it sure would be nice if my bed were in the middle of the room."

We heard what sounded like a thousand squeaky voices whispering, countless little feet padding about on the carpet, and then a loud THUD as something heavy in Heather's room hit the ground. She opened the door and we peered in. Her bed had moved.

I got an anxious feeling.

"Isn't that amazing?!" said Heather. Tienna, Shane, and I looked at each other. Heather's ghosts sure did sound like an army of hamsters. "Okay, now come into my room for a second."

"Heather . . ." I began. There were no ghosts here.

"Hush, Teddy!" Heather ushered us in. Tienna and Shane glanced around, worried. They knew, too.

"Heather"—I began again—"there's something we need to tell you." Oh geez. How was I supposed to tell Heather that her hamster had been the mastermind of a plan to eat everyone's brains?

"Shush, Teddy!" She closed the door behind us. "Boy,

it sure would be nice for me and my friends to have some snacks," she stated.

Once again there was a flurry of whispering, plus cackling and what sounded like a tornado moving through the kitchen downstairs. Plates clattered. A glass shattered. Squeaky cursing followed. The fridge slammed shut. The "ghosts" huffed and puffed up the stairs and then there was a THUD right outside the door.

Heather peeked into the hallway.

An echoing squeaky laugh rang out from behind the walls followed by the scratching of a thousand claws from all around us.

"Heather, you don't have ghosts." I backed away from the plates. "You have hamsters." We had to get out of there!

"What?!"

"It's true," Shane said. "Evil talking hamsters!"

"WHAT?!"

Tienna grabbed the heaviest book she could find off Heather's bookshelf. "Everybody grab a hamster-smasher!"

"There will be NO hamster-smashing in this house!" Heather snatched the book out of Tienna's hands.

"Milk would be fine, too!" Shane backed into the middle of the room.

Milk. Gross.

"We don't drink milk! N-n-none of this makes sense!" Heather's face flushed. Her voice turned shrill. "I don't like this game, guys!"

"It's true, Heather." I walked over to Scrabbles's cage

and picked it up. "And it all started with Scrabbles."

I felt a warm fuzzy thing land on my shoulder and something cold at my throat. Whiskers tickled my cheek and a furious squeaky voice whispered in my ear.

HAMSTERS!

"Oh my gosh, look at his little cape and helmet!" Heather squealed in glee. "It's ADORABLE!"

"You honor me, my queen," the hamster on my shoulder squeaked.

"I'm your queen?" Heather clapped and grinned.

I gently put the hamster cage down and turned so I could look in Heather's mirror. The rodent on my shoulder was bigger and beefier than the others we'd seen and looked ANGRY.

"Please don't kill me," I squeaked. I dropped my camera.

"No promises, Pukey Bear!"

There was a horrendous cracking noise as Tienna broke Heather's desk chair and held one of its legs like a baseball bat.

Turn a little to your right, Teddy. I think I can get him!

"One step forward and I start slicing, ogress!"

"Please—no slicing!" I squeaked.

"Heather!" Shane tugged at Heather's sleeve. "Do you have any cheese?"

"This isn't the time for a snack!" Tienna snarled.

"No—cheese is just solid milk, right? It might work!"

"You want to throw CHEESE at the ham—"

"ALL OF YOU CALM DOWN!" Heather shouted.

Heather picked up one of the apple slices off the plate and offered it to the hamster. "What's your name?"

"I am known as Biscuit, my queen."

"Biscuit! Oh my gosh, I love it!" Heather squealed.

"Heather," I whined. "Help!"

"Right! Sorry, Teddy. Can you please let my friend go?"

"But he is the milk-sprayer! The DESPOILER! He has reduced the great Scrabbles to a mere fuzzy shell." The unseen hamsters in the walls wailed. "He ruined all our plans."

"What plans?" Heather moved a little closer with the apple slice.

"We were to take the place of those that wronged you so that you may have friends."

"By eating their brains!" Tienna snarled. She gripped the chair leg so hard her knuckles were white.

"That's not true, is it Biscuit?"

"It . . . it is, my queen."

"But that's horrible."

"We did it for the greater good." Biscuit threw back his head and let loose a squeaky howl. "Praise be to Heather, provider of apples!"

"What are you DOING?!" Heather yelled. She wrestled the chair leg away from Tienna. "It's just a hamster!"

I rubbed at my throat where the hamster axe had been and backed into the middle of the room with Shane. GEEZ that was close!

"It was gonna hurt Teddy!"

"It was just scared. Hamsters are kind, gentle, loving creatures and they would NEVER hurt anyone."

Tienna broke off another chair leg with a CRACK. "You were brainwashed last week during the whole hamster thing so I'll cut you some slack, but these hamsters are NOT gentle."

"You're a brute," Heather stated. "Get out of my house!"

"Heather . . ." This was an awful situation, but I didn't want my friends to fight. "Please, let us explain."

"Go home, Teddy," Heather whispered. She picked up Biscuit, who was recovering from his thwacking. "We'll talk tomorrow."

"Come on, guys," Tienna snarled. "Hamster-Girl says we need to leave."

Heather stood there silently.

"Let's go," Shane said. He tugged on my sleeve. "She'll be fine. The hamsters would never hurt her."

I looked back as we filed out of the room. Biscuit glared at me with an intense, burning hatred.

We saw ourselves out. It felt like a thousand beady little eyes were burrowing into the back of my skull as we left.

"Tienna!" Heather shouted from her bedroom window.

We turned.

"That was my grandma's chair." Heather slammed the window shut.

Tienna blushed. She looked at the chair leg still in her hand then set it gently on the front steps.

We walked back to my house in silence.

Duggy Acts REALLY Weird

"Enthralling," Duggy said. "And then what happened?"

Shane, Duggy, and I had gathered in front of my locker for our morning hangout session.

I shrugged. "Well, then we left."

"Beguiling."

Shane looked up from his sketchbook. "Okay, Duggy, WHAT is going on with you? You're using really big words, you're not hyperactive, and you still smell like cheese."

Duggy DID still have a fromage-y funk. But if Duggy wanted to chill out and learn new big words, who was I to judge?

Nothing goes on, friends.

I am Duggy.

Okay, that was a little odd.

Shane looked at me and raised his eyebrows as if to say, "See?!"

I was about to agree with Shane, but I spotted Heather walking toward us. She had a hamster ball cradled in her arms. As she approached, she sniffed the air and gave Duggy a withering glare. He smiled. She rolled her eyes and thrust the hamster ball toward me.

"Teddy, we would like to apologize." Inside the ball was Biscuit. I backed up against the locker.

Fear not, Pukey Bear, I come in peace.

"This is Biscuit, the greatest of nibblers. He's sworn to never allow anyone except me to touch Scrabbles. He was just carrying out his duty." She patted the hamster ball. Biscuit glared at me with his beady little eyes. "My hamsters told me everything. About Scrabbles, the great ceremony, everything. I . . . I can see why Tienna acted the way she did. I'm sorry for overreacting."

"It's okay," I said. Wait a minute . . .

I grabbed my phone and snapped a photo, but all it showed was an adorable little fuzzball in a cape. Not evidence-worthy. Darn. I tried to record a video instead, but hitting the button crashed the whole app.

Dad's phone really was old.

Cute

Fuzzy-wuzzy

Not in any way threatening

Heather patted the hamster ball. "And you and your brothers and sisters are sorry for . . . ?"

Biscuit crossed his little arms and pouted. "I apologize for attempting to rid this world of the milk-bringer."

"And . . . ?" Heather prompted.

"And we, the children of Scrabbles the great all-father, promise not to directly harm you, your family, or the death-that-meows that haunts your home."

RELIEF!

"However, we are not happy about it."

"Biscuit! You promised."

"We shall never directly harm you, Teddy, but know this"—Biscuit clenched his little fist and waved it in my general direction—"we shall never forgive! Your garden will be nothing but holes! Your locker shall forever smell of wood shavings! Any small dark food you encounter henceforth may be hamster poop! WILD RICE, RAISINS, AND CHOCOLATE CHIPS SHALL NEVER BE SAFE AGAIN, PUKEY BEAR!"

Well, that explained all the holes in our yard.

Definitely not gophers.

Heather stuffed the hamster ball into her backpack. The squeaking and swearing continued, muffled. She smiled apologetically.

"We'll work on it, Teddy. They REALLY don't like you."

"You were not lying. That domesticated cricetid speaks!" Duggy cried. "And with such accomplished eloquence. Astounding!"

We all turned and looked at Duggy.

"I desire to see it again," he said. "I must take notes."

Okay, Duggy was acting REALLY weird. He knew about the hamsters. He'd had conversations with the hamsters. He'd made a DEAL with the hamsters. Also, Duggy HATES taking notes. What the heck?!

I was about to say something, but I heard Milton's pre-tantrum voice behind me.

"I don't wanna!"

We turned to see Martin and Milton walking toward us. Milton did NOT look happy.

"It's okay, Milton," Martin said. He gently ushered

Milton toward us. As they approached, Milton scooted behind me and buried his face in my hoodie.

Martin heaved a heavy sigh.

"What's wrong?" I asked. I tried to peel Milton loose, but he just tightened his grip. Geez this kid was strong.

"Milton says that Duggy scared him yesterday." Martin tried to pry Milton off me without success.

Duggy narrowed his eyes and stared at Milton hungrily.

Wait . . . Hungrily?

Milton unburied his face from my hoodie to glare at Duggy then buried it again.

"It's just Duggy, Milton," Shane said. "Sure, he's weird, but he's harmless." He poked Duggy with his pencil. Duggy smiled and chuckled. "Really weird."

"Milton, what did Duggy do to scare you?" Heather asked.

Milton stayed buried.

Oh geez. I had no idea what to do here. Milton was like a snotty Mr. Fuzzikins. Maybe a reassuring pat on the shoulder? Yeah. Maybe that'd help.

Pat. Pat.

"You believe me, don't you, Teddy?"

"Believe you?" I asked.

Milton risked a glance at Duggy. He motioned me to lean down then whispered in my ear. "Duggy's a monster!"

Duggy's eyes widened slightly.

"Milton, you're not wearing your hearing aids," Martin said, exasperated. "We're at school now, so a deal's a deal." Milton looked miserable, but he let Martin put them on.

NOT DUGGY!

Milton tore out his hearing aids and sprinted away. He bounced off Ms. Mint, scrambled into the learning resource room, slammed the door, and locked it.

"Goodness me," Ms. Mint said. "Is everything okay, Martin? I guess I need to go get my keys!"

"I'm so sorry, Ms. Mint." Martin ran over and knocked on the door.

I bent down to pick the powder-blue hearing aids off the floor and noticed they were squealing. Maybe that squealing sound was hurting him? I'd hate that in my ears all day. Geez. Poor Milton.

We're tangenting, Teddy!

I held a hearing aid up to my ear.

Duggy was a monster.

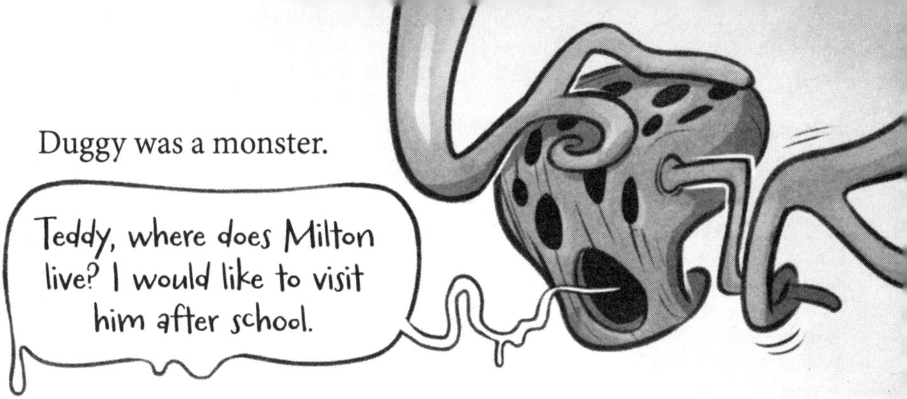

"Teddy, where does Milton live? I would like to visit him after school."

I heard Duggy's voice, but instead of speaking (I didn't see a mouth), the monster cranked a wheel on a strange box. It was made from something that looked like driftwood.

Or bones . . .

"Duggy, what are YOU doin' here?!"

"Get out of here, you smelly little monster!"

The ... the THING slithered its way along the hallways. It reeked of cheese.

I stood there, eyes wide, frozen to the spot.

Duggy was a monster ...

"Tienna, that was too much," Shane said sternly.

"That was REALLY mean, Tienna." Heather put her hands on her hips. "But since you're here, me and Biscuit want to apologize."

Duggy... was a MONSTER.

"You brought a hamster to school?!" Tienna scowled. "What is WRONG with you?!"

The Duggy monster inched along the corridor like some awful alien caterpillar.

"I wish to apologize, Tienna, foe of Scrufflechops," said Biscuit.

The Duggy thing slithered around the corner.

"Of COURSE you brought a hamster back to school!" Tienna threw her hands in the air. "You know what? I can't handle this right now." She turned to me. "What's wrong with the Milton gremlin?"

My legs came back to life. I ignored Tienna and ran over to Martin, who was still knocking on the door to the learning assistance room.

Oh my gosh, Milton was right!

DUGGY WAS A MONSTER.

"MARTIN!"

"Oh good." Martin smiled. "Maybe you can help me get him out of here."

"Martin, Milton was . . ." Why did I always have to explain things like brain-eating hamsters and monsters that can only be seen with hearing aids? It's really hard!

AGH!

"Milton was what, Teddy?"

"Milton was right," I whispered in my cousin's ear. "Duggy's a monster."

Martin sighed. "Teddy, don't play games. No, he's not. There's no such thing as monsters."

"Martin, you have to listen to me—"

"STOP IT!" Martin shouted.

I had NEVER heard Martin shout before.

"Teddy"—Martin took a deep breath—"did you pick up his hearing aids?"

I slipped one of the hearing aids into my pocket. "I only found one," I lied.

"Great. Just great."

Milton's teary voice echoed through the door.

"Teddy, I'm scared! You believe me, right?"

"Yeah, Milton, I believe you."

Martin rubbed at his eyes. "Look, Teddy, if you wanna play games with Milton then why don't you walk him home after school?"

"I don't think..." I began. Martin glanced back at me. His eyes were red. He seemed really tired all of a sudden.

"Actually... yeah," I said. "Sure. I'd be fine with that." I was a little surprised that I meant it. "Hear that, Milton? I'll walk you home from school today."

Milton held Mr. Bear to his ear then nodded and sniffled. "Thanks, Teddy."

I definitely didn't think I was the best person to keep Milton safe.

He was almost dog food the last time!

But since he and I were the only ones who could see whatever Duggy had turned into, I had to try. He was my little cousin, after all.

This was exactly the kind of thing I was looking for! If I could get a picture of whatever this . . . this THING was, my parents would have to move us back to Kamloops.

I couldn't keep calling it just "the thing," though. It had to have a name. Something like the cheese snake? Maybe the cheddar caterpillar? The slimy sentinel?

Teddy! Tangent!

Maybe just the worm. Yeah. The worm.

The worm slithered through the hall. It was so tall that its head scraped the ceiling and so long that people kept tripping over its snaky tail. No one seemed to realize that there was a huge cheesy monstrosity roaming the halls, though. Every time they tripped, they'd shrug and carry on. I was the only one who could see it. Well, I guess Milton could see it, too. I lined up the camera and snapped a picture.

Click.

But the screen only showed what looked like Duggy in the crowded Ravensbee hallway. No monster. I'd have to get a picture of this thing some other way.

"I don't see any monster, Teddy." Heather patted me on the shoulder. "It's just Duggy. Are you feeling okay?"

Of course it was just Duggy. It had always been just Duggy. That was the problem! HAD it always been Duggy? Had Duggy ALWAYS been some awful alien worm-thing? But then why had he been acting so strange lately? What if Duggy had been—

"TEDDY!"

I nearly jumped to the ceiling and then whipped around. Tienna stood there nonchalantly. She chuckled. Shane stood beside her.

"We've gotta work on that jumpiness, buddy. Wanna come on a run around the field with me? That always helps clear my head."

Shane glanced at the phone in my hand. "What are you taking pictures of?"

"Teddy thinks Duggy's a monster," Heather said in a friendly and understanding tone. "He was trying to get a picture. Isn't that nice?" She patted me on the head.

"We already know he's a monster," Tienna sneered.

"We don't need a picture."

"I think he really means it, Tienna." Shane looked down the hall at Duggy. "Just looks like Duggy to me, though."

"How come you can see it then, Teddy?" Tienna asked.

"I think it's Milton's hearing aids." I fiddled with the device, trying to fit it in my ear, but it wasn't designed for me. "They do something to—"

Tienna snatched the hearing aid with two bony fingers and held it up to her ear. Her eyes went wide, then she turned and grabbed Shane's ear.

"Ow! Tienna! Personal space! That thing is covered in earwax!" Shane batted at Tienna's hands as she held it against his ear, then his eyes went wide too as he looked down the hallway.

Without a word he handed the hearing aid to Heather, who gingerly held it up to her ear. She gasped in shock.

"Teddy, this is exactly the kind of thing you're looking for!" Heather exclaimed.

"I know," I said and smiled. Evidence!

Tienna laughed and slapped one of my hands. Ow.

133

"High five, Teddy! You're a monster hunter extraordinaire! So how are we gonna get a picture of this thing?"

The door to Monsieur Lambert's room opened behind us. "Oh! My tiny friends! I wondered who was making so much noise."

"Sorry, Monsieur Lambert," Tienna said. "We're just kind of excited is all!"

We looked at each other.

"Yeah," I replied. "Every morning."

"Oh good." He sighed. "I have been worried."

"Why?" Heather asked.

"Well . . . Has Duggy seemed . . . odd to you lately?"

"Maybe a little," Shane said.

"He hasn't stopped by to play cards this week, and when I said good morning to him, he seemed not to know who I was. Last week he was his usual chipper self. This week he is a stranger."

Unease crept up from the pit of my stomach.

Last week Duggy HAD been his chipper self. This week he was completely different.

Unease turned to anxiety and clawed at my innards.

"We'll . . . uh . . ." Shane struggled for a moment. "We'll talk to him, Monsieur Lambert. I think he's just a little off this week."

"Merci. Please tell him I miss playing cards with him." He ducked back into his office and shut the door.

Shane and I looked at each other. My gut wrenched.

Shane looked worried. What if that . . . that THING wasn't actually Duggy?

What if that thing had REPLACED Duggy?

"So like I was saying, how are we gonna get a picture of this thing?" Tienna asked.

"A picture?" My heart pounded and my breaths came sharp and quick. "Who cares about a picture?! What about Duggy?"

"What are you talking about, Teddy?" Tienna rolled her eyes.

"Tienna . . ." Shane put his hand on her shoulder. "That's not Duggy! Last week he was completely normal, but this week he's been acting TOTALLY out of character."

"And he smells like a cheesy sewer," Heather added.

Tienna rolled her eyes. "So?"

"So where's the REAL Duggy?" Shane asked.

Tienna sneered. "Who cares?"

"Who cares? WHO CARES?!" I shouted. I didn't give a darn if this wasn't my line. My friend was missing!

"I CARE! What if he's been kidnapped?" I bit my nails.

"What if he's tied up in some basement somewhere, cold and alone with no one to talk to and whatever that THING is plans to eat his body for dinner but keep his head separate to sew it onto the body of some scruffy stray dog and show it off in an alien zoo?! WHAT IF IT'S GONNA DO THE SAME TO US?!"

"Or what if it plans to use Duggy's organs to season alien soup?" came a voice from Heather's backpack.

"Biscuit"—Heather peered into her backpack—"don't say such horrible things!"

"Apologies, my lady," the hamster cackled.

"Hamsters don't get to have opinions," Tienna snarled. She grabbed my hand out of my mouth. "Don't do that, Teddy. Geez you're a champion at playing 'ain't it awful.' Why should we care about that little weasel? He was gonna feed us to the hamsters!"

Tienna glared at me. There was a moment of silence.

"We need to find the real Duggy," Shane finally said. "That thing doesn't know that we can see it, so let's follow it after school."

"Good idea," Heather agreed. She zipped up her backpack. "Let's meet at the soccer field."

"We've got a plan, then." Shane nodded and turned to Tienna. "I know you haven't forgiven Duggy, but—"

"Duggy is a slimy little jerk, and I'm NEVER going to forgive him for what happened with the hamsters."

My heart sank. Tienna was my friend. Duggy was my friend, too. Was I going to have to choose between the two of them?

Why do friendships have to be so darn complicated?!

"BUT," she continued, "you guys are right. KIND of right. I don't like Duggy, but I don't want anything to eat him." For a split second, Tienna's sneer slipped, and she looked worried instead of angry. "We gotta find him."

Relief! I smiled. "Thanks, Tienna."

"Besides"—Tienna smiled grimly—"if that thing turns out to be dangerous, you guys are gonna need my help."

Mr. Bear

I made my way down the primary wing of Ravensbee. It had that weird funky school smell of apple juice, yogurt, and old sandwich.

Gross.

I peered around the door into the kindergarten. Mrs. Rose glanced up. "Oh hello! You must be Teddy." She smiled warmly. "You look just like Martin."

Ha!

"Um, yeah. I'm here to pick up Milton. I'm walking him home today."

"Oh!" Mrs. Rose looked confused. "I'm afraid Martin already picked Milton up."

That was weird. Oh geez, I hoped Martin wasn't mad at me for siding with Milton earlier . . .

"He actually came by just after lunch. Said something about a family emergency. He sounded a little strange, too. Maybe he's coming down with something."

Well THAT wasn't good.

"Also . . ." Mrs. Rose looked off to the side, embarrassed. "If you could let Milton's mother know that he managed to sneak his hearing aid out on me again." She reached into one of her deep pockets and pulled out one of Milton's powder-blue hearing aids. "I'll hold on to it until tomorrow, but I just wanted to make sure she knows it's safe."

I thanked Mrs. Rose and made my way outside.

I looked around the field and playground for my friends.

I didn't see them, but sitting, sullen and dejected, in the middle of the field was Mr. Bear. I ran over and picked up Milton's stuffy. It was wet from the rain. I got anxious. Milton would NEVER leave Mr. Bear behind.

Tienna came around the side of the school and jogged up to me. "Come on, Teddy! I saw Duggy walk-

ing off toward the northern trailhead. Where's Milton?"

"Martin picked him up."

"Oh, well, let's go, then. I don't wanna fall too far behind the worm-thing."

"But . . . it's Mr. Bear." I brushed some of the rain off his fur. "Milton loves this thing. He thinks Mr. Bear can replace his hearing aids. He wouldn't just leave him behind."

"Kids forget stuff all the time, Teddy."

"I guess . . ." I gently packed Mr. Bear into my backpack. Tienna was probably right. Milton was just a little kid.

"Now come on. Let's go!" Tienna tugged on my arm.

I took a deep breath.

Nope. Still anxious.

We crouched in a bush across the street from Duggy's house. At least I was fairly sure it was Duggy's house. It was a pretty, single-story home painted a rustic brown. Flowers of every shade festooned the large garden and the walkway up to the door. A mailbox painted to look like a dog with its jaws open wide had the name "Copelind" brightly written on its side.

Tienna had lost patience with waiting and had dashed across the street to knock on the door, but no one had answered. She peered through the front windows, peeked over the fence into the backyard, and then ran back to us.

"No one home?" Shane asked.

"No," Tienna replied. "I don't think the worm's in there anymore."

"Maybe it left through the back?" Heather suggested.

"Why would it do that?" Shane asked.

I looked beyond the house and the fenced backyard. I could just make out the roof of a crude shack in the woods. The misty, rainy, DANGEROUS woods. Oh no . . .

Just say it, Teddy!

145

"Duggy said he was building a fort," I got out.

A muffled squeak echoed from Heather's backpack. "My queen, this is not safe. Let us go home!"

"You're lucky you don't get punted into the woods, you fluffy rat," Tienna growled. "Well, the worm's not in the house. Let's go check out Duggy's fort."

Shane and Heather hurried after Tienna into Duggy's backyard. Somehow staying here alone seemed like a worse idea, so I chased after them. The gate leading to the forest was almost hidden beside a huge woodpile. Someone had been using an old axe to cut a LOT of wood.

"Looks like they're stocking up for the winter already," Shane mused.

Winter? WINTER?! This place was already cold enough and it was barely autumn!

We walked through the back gate, and it latched behind us with a click. The main trail meandered through the forest back toward town, but deeper in the woods along a thin path was a small hut made of scrap plywood with a dirty old curtain for a door.

Dozens of small, unmarked trails rambled off into the woods beyond the fort. I sniffed. The air smelled of cheese.

Heather's backpack squeaked. "My queen, this trail is not safe! We have sensed the presence of this beast before. It smells of ancient death. It is known as the trail wyrm."

"If it smells dangerous, why didn't you say something back at school?" Heather asked. "Duggy's been cheesy all week!"

"The entire school reeks of fromage, my lady. All children are smelly little beasts that bathe in the devil's drink. How was I to know?"

Tienna rolled her eyes. "It's just a fort, you stupid hamster!"

"Let me out, my queen. Let me prove my worth."

"Okay, Biscuit, but be careful!" Heather unzipped her backpack and popped the lid off the hamster ball.

"What are you doing?!" Tienna shouted. "Don't let it loose!" She scrambled after the hamster, but Biscuit scurried into the fort with a high-pitched panting noise. His little claws sprayed leaves and dirt around as he scrambled under the plywood.

"He's just trying to help!" Heather shouted.

"Help?!" Tienna seethed. "They tried to kill us all!"

Shane put a hand on Tienna's shoulder. "Maybe he can find something we can't see?"

"Tienna, we don't have a lot of options," I said. "If Biscuit can help, why not let him? We have to find Duggy."

"I know . . ." Tienna closed her eyes. We stood in silence for a few moments. The rain dripped. "It's just . . . I'm worried too, okay?"

"I thought you hated Duggy," Heather pointed out.

"I don't hate him, Heather." Tienna crossed her arms and looked off into the forest. Rain dripped from her hat. "I was just angry with him. And now I'm worried about him."

The Den

Biscuit pointed at a patch of dirt wall that looked like all the rest, then he scurried at full speed toward it. I thought he was going to break his neck, but he ran through it like it wasn't there. Then Biscuit disappeared. It was an illusion!

Shane's eyes went wide. "Oh my gosh!" He stuck his hand through the dirt illusion. "It's like a hologram!"

It looked like it was there, but it wasn't. Just like Duggy. I held Milton's hearing aid up to my ear, and the illusion disappeared. In its place was a tunnel about five feet wide. It spiraled down. Just beyond, I saw Biscuit, illuminated by a sickening purple light, beckoning us.

I handed the hearing aid to Shane. "Oh cool!" he said.

"It does not go far," Biscuit squeaked. "Come! The cheese-monster is not here."

"What do you mean, he's not here?" Tienna scurried into the tunnel, ignoring the illusion completely. "Where else could he be?"

"Maybe he went somewhere else?" Shane ducked into the tunnel with the hearing aid.

"Biscuit, don't go too far!" Heather joined him.

I bit my nails. This was a terrible idea. We were gonna go down the tunnel and then the worm was gonna find us andthenitwasgonnatearourskinoffwithitsclawsandeat—

Tienna's hand shot out of the illusion and tore my fingers out of my mouth.

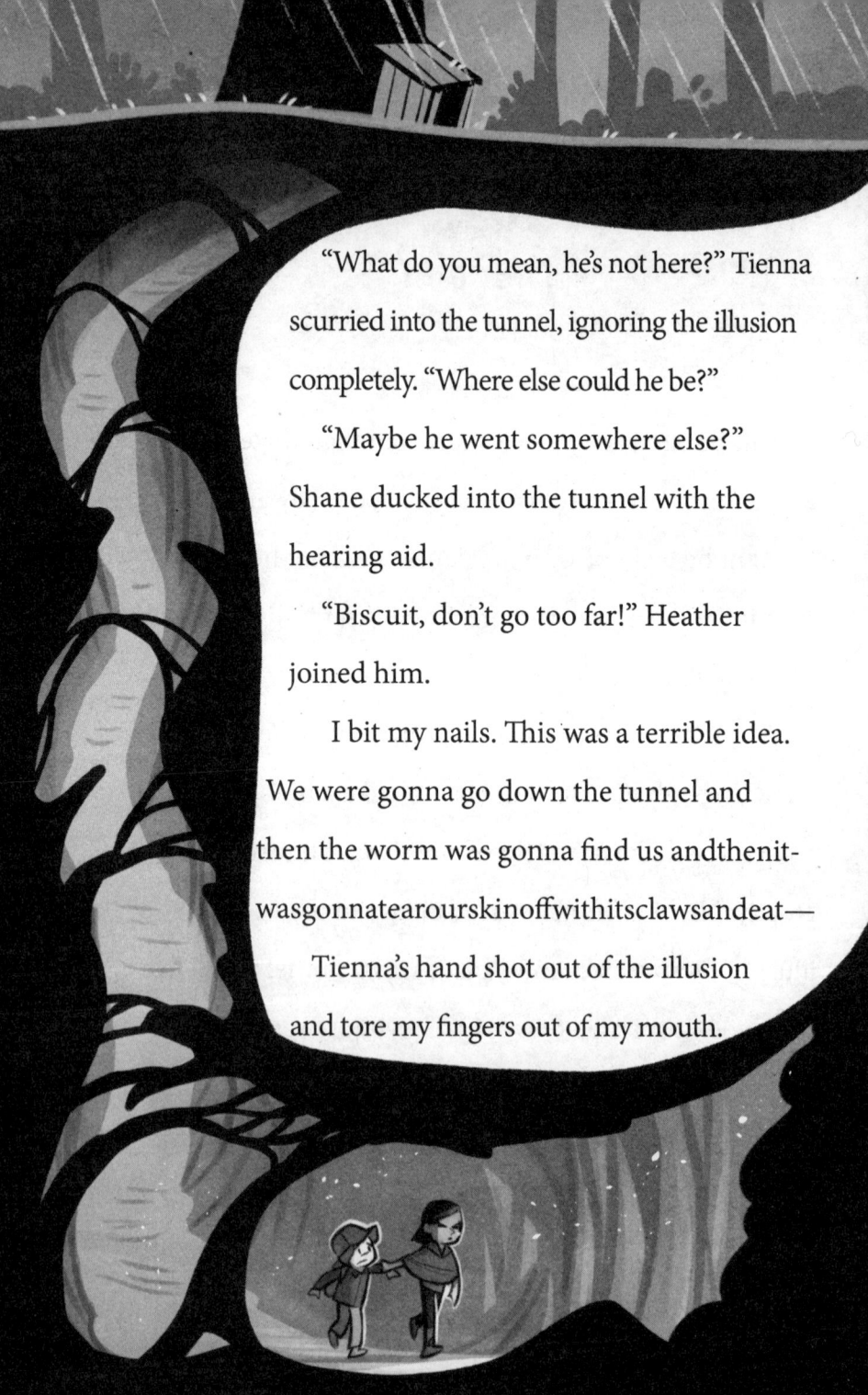

"Don't do that, Teddy. We're not splitting up. Come on." She pulled me into the tunnel, and we slowly made our way deep underground.

The tunnel absolutely REEKED of cheese and an awful slime coated everything. Our shoes squelched and schlorped. We spiraled down for a short while then emerged into a large chamber.

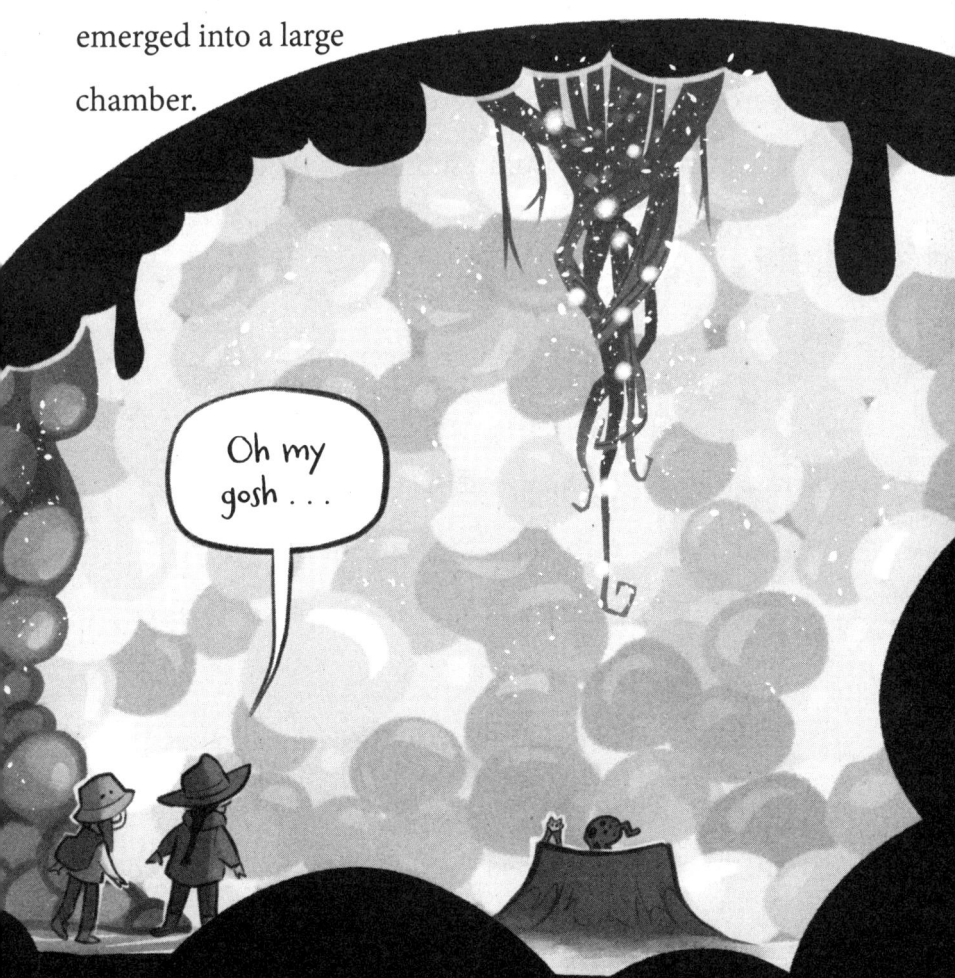

Tree roots hung from the ceiling about twenty feet above our heads. Thousands of little glowing bugs moved around the roots, turning them into massive snaky chandeliers. In the middle of the room was a raised dirt platform about the size of a coffee table. The worm's bone box sat there. Everything was coated in slime. All around the chamber were thousands of slimy bubbles made from a substance that kind of looked like glass. Some were small (hamster-sized?) and some were larger. The larger ones were... They were...

Duggy-sized.

Oh no.

"Be wary, my queen. This place stinks of evil," Biscuit chittered.

Shane had already run up to the larger spheres and was peering into them. "They're covered in condensation," he said as he wiped the bubble clear. "The big ones are all filled with animals! Deer and rabbits and stuff!"

"This one has a squirrel in it," Tienna said. She frantically searched through the bubbles. She had that worried look on her face that I had every day. Tienna was anxious.

"These ones have birds." Shane wiped his now-slimy hand on his pants. "These ones all have lizards . . . bugs . . . flowers. It's like it's collecting samples or something."

I walked over to the bone box. There were tiny holes carved in the surface, kind of like a flute or ocarina.

"What's that, Teddy?" Heather whispered behind me. I jumped a little.

"I think it's how the thing speaks. Back at school it turned the wheel and Duggy's voice came out."

"Should we try it?" Heather reached toward it.

"I'm not sure that's a good idea," I said quickly. Fiddle with an alien monster's literal voice box? Absolutely not!

"Your cowardice is legendary, Pukey Bear!" Biscuit scrambled up onto the table, huffing and puffing. "Allow me to assist, my queen." The hamster grabbed the wheel and cranked.

We jumped as an awful wail filled the room. It was a wordless moan and it sounded just...

like...

Duggy.

Waaaaaaauuuuuu...

The floating lights pulsed as the moan followed the crank of the wheel.

Uuuuuuaaaaaaaaaa...

"DUGGY?!" Tienna ran over. "What is THAT?!" She looked worried. We all did.

"It's what it was using to talk," I said. I backed away from the table. "I don't think it has a mouth." I slapped my hands to my ears to block the noise.

Shane reached out and put a finger over one of the holes. The Duggy moan changed vowels.

Tienna lashed out to knock Biscuit away, but he scurried out of reach. The moaning stopped. Tienna turned and walked back toward the tunnel. She had tears in her eyes. There was a moment of silence and then Tienna let loose a piercing, vicious swear. She grabbed the sphere with the squirrel in it and threw it as hard as she could against the table in the center of the room. The ball popped like a water balloon, spraying liquid everywhere. The squirrel slithered out on a trail of slime. After a moment it shakily got to its feet then dashed away.

Tienna sniffed and wiped her eyes. Heather reached out to put her hand on Tienna's shoulder then pulled back. Shane furrowed his brow, but then he peered into the wall of bubbles and his eyes went wide.

"GUYS! DUGGY!"

Tienna scrambled over to the pile of slime bubbles and tried her best to roll them away. We joined her and soon cleared them all.

I tore at the bubble with my bare hands. It was like trying to cut a steak with a spoon. It was . . . meaty.

"Out of the way, Teddy!" Tienna had grabbed one of the dry tree roots from the chandelier. After a few stabs, the bubble popped. There was an overwhelming stench of cheese as strange alien goop sloshed everywhere and Duggy slithered across the slimy floor. He sat up immediately, gasping for breath, eyes wide. He looked around at us then wept in relief.

You STUPID little dingus! I hate you so much!

Duggy hugged Tienna back. After a second Tienna realized what she was doing (hugging Duggy the BETRAYER) and shoved him away.

"It's just like you to get yourself into a stupid situation where we have to risk our lives, DUGGY!" Tienna kicked several of the bubbles then stalked back to the tunnel entrance where she stood with a scowl and crossed arms.

"Duggy, what happened to you?" Shane demanded.

Duggy opened and closed his mouth like he was trying to talk, but no sound came out. Just a breathy whisper.

"Duggy, what's wrong?" I asked.

Duggy pointed to his neck. We saw a thin red line across his throat like a tiny surgical scar. More breathy noises rattled out of his mouth.

Oh man . . . That wasn't good.

"He can't talk," I whispered. Anxiety clawed its way into my throat. Was that gonna happen to us? I LIKED my voice! I broke a stick off the root Tienna had used to pop Duggy's slimy prison. "Write it out, Duggy."

Duggy snatched the stick and scribbled in the dirt.

I looked over at the box that the worm-thing used to talk and felt sick to my stomach.

Teddy, we need to LEAVE!

"Why?" Shane asked, always curious.

Wants to make new things, Duggy wrote.

New things? NEW THINGS? WHAT?!

Teddy, we need to leave RIGHT NOW!

"Guys, let's get out of here!" I tugged at Duggy's arm.

Duggy nodded and scrambled to his feet. We all hurried toward the tunnel.

"WAIT!" Biscuit squeaked. He held up a claw and his little nose sniffed rapidly.

I Mess Up

A sound like Dad dragging a wet garbage bag across the garage floor echoed down the tunnel. We looked around. The only things here were the awful bubbles and the dirt platform. There weren't any hiding spots!

"In the bubbles!" Shane whispered.

Shane, Heather, and Duggy squirmed their way between the fleshy alien goo-pods, but I hesitated. They were so . . . slimy.

Gross!

Tienna shoved me into the pile of bubbles with an awful SCHLORP. It was like being hugged by an elephant covered in dish soap.

CHEESY dish soap!

I gagged.

Tienna squeezed in beside me and gave me an angry glare. "Teddy, if you throw up, I'm going to feed you to the monster. Get it together."

Yeah, because it's that easy, TIENNA!

I choked back both my angry retort and a load of puke. We waited, motionless, as the slithery dragging noise got louder . . . and louder . . . and then . . .

The worm oozed past us toward the platform. Light from the root chandelier glistened on its rubbery skin. As it passed the platform, it looked down at the burst bubble that Tienna had thrown. It glanced over at Duggy's broken prison. The slimy filling had blended with the rest of the goo in the room, but the pieces of broken bubble sat out in the open like used rags.

We held our breath.

The worm swiveled its long slimy snake neck to calmly look around the room. Little skin flaps opened and closed as it took a deep breath. The monster didn't seem to do anything all that fast. Its tail flicked back and forth excitedly.

Duggy started to shake. Tienna slowly (and quietly) picked up a small rock from the floor.

As soon as the worm had turned its head again, Tienna tossed the rock toward the back of the chamber. It landed with a muffled schlorp amidst the bubbles. The worm calmly slithered toward the noise.

Tienna tugged on my hoodie. She motioned with

her head toward the tunnel. With the worm distracted, we could get away!

Shane and Heather eased out of the bubble pile and sneaked back toward the tunnel. Biscuit sat on Heather's shoulder, hamster axe at the ready. He kept his eyes on the worm and beckoned us with his paw.

Tienna gently dragged me into the open. Duggy, his eyes wide, moved into the tunnel and Tienna followed him. I tiptoed after them but glanced back at the worm. It was searching through the stack of bubbles.

Teddy!

It's not disguised!

Teddy!

Now's not the time! Who cares if it's not disguised?!

22
STUPID AUTOMATIC FLASH!
SCREECH

I'd said before that the worm didn't have a mouth.

I was wrong.

The maw gaped at least six feet wide and was filled with thousands upon thousands of slimy needle-teeth.

The screech rattled my brain and threatened to knock my eyeballs loose. The worm covered its eyes with its tentacles and reared back in pain.

Tienna ran back down the tunnel, grabbed my shoulder, and pulled me forward. The ground swayed under my feet.

We scrambled out into the open then sprinted through the rain. A horrid squelching punctuated by deep, wet panting echoed from underground. It was right behind us!

Tienna and I dove over a fallen log (well, Tienna dove, I kinda tripped). I tried to get to my feet, but Tienna put her hand on my shoulder and a single finger to her lips.

The forest was silent . . .

But I could still make out the awful, slimy breathing of the worm.

I peeked under the log. Through the undergrowth and mushrooms I could just make out its long, rubbery body. It weaved its head back and forth like a cobra.

Without a sound it dropped to the ground and began to leisurely slither, bending around trees and over logs. Searching.

Tienna slowly, silently picked up a rock.

I held my breath.

The rain whispered.

There was the faintest swishing of wet grass and soggy leaves . . . and then . . .

Off in the forest, Biscuit let loose a rolling squeaky trill.

The hand withdrew, and we heard the soft rustling of the worm slithering away.

Another squeak echoed through the forest, this time further away. Then again, even further.

Biscuit had saved us!

Tienna risked a glance over the log then pulled me to my feet. We ran back to Duggy's yard where Shane, Duggy, and Heather were waiting. Tienna slammed the gate behind us. Soon after, Biscuit came scurrying back.

Heather picked up the hamster and squeezed him. "Oh, Biscuit, you're so brave!"

"It was nothing, my queen." Biscuit preened. "Such bravery is common among your children."

"Who cares about the hamster?" Tienna cut in. "What the heck happened in the tunnel?! What was that bright flash of light?"

"I don't know!" Shane exclaimed. "Whatever it was, it really ticked off that monster."

I peeked down at my dad's phone. I had a perfect

picture of the worm.

I had the evidence I needed to convince my parents. Now what was I supposed to tell my friends?

They don't need to know, Teddy.

But they're our friends!

They'll blame you, Teddy. The thing only chased you because YOU wanted to take a picture!

I guess...

"I dunno either," I lied. "But let's get out of here."

I had lied to my friends. I was gross. Ugh.

"Where are we gonna go?" Tienna asked. "No offense, Duggy, but I don't feel like hanging out at your house when it's, like, ten feet from that thing's lair."

Duggy clung to me. "Don't worry," I told him, "we're not gonna leave you alone."

"Well," said Shane, thinking out loud, "the comic shop's close by."

Nerd's Roost

"Yeah, pretty much," said Tienna, shrugging. Shane poked her in the ribs. Tienna punched him in the shoulder and he winced.

"I'm sorry, Candice," Shane said. "We've . . . um . . ."

"We've had a long day," Heather cut in. "We got a little lost on the trails."

"Yeah," Tienna agreed. "Just a little turned around."

Candice raised an eyebrow and leaned over the counter to stare us in the eyes one by one. "Lost? How? You didn't go OFF the marked trails, did you? Even a little bit?"

"Absolutely not!" Shane was aghast.

Well, that's kinda disappointing.

You miss out on so much if you stick to the marked trails.

"You go on unmarked trails?!" Shane was horrified.

"The best paths are off the main trail! And the REALLY good ones are unmarked. There's a shortcut filled with purple mushrooms that takes you all the way from the northern trailhead to the train yard."

Shane looked puzzled. "That doesn't make sense. That would take you through the lake."

"And I've NEVER seen purple mushrooms here before," Heather added.

"Try it some time. If you head north off the main trail from the northern trailhead, you'll be able to spot the shortcut. Especially at night. So what? You thought you'd just hang out here after getting lost in the woods?"

"Well, yeah." Shane shrugged.

"Wouldn't be my first choice is all, but I guess you guys are a little young for the pub." Candice smiled. "Oh, by the way, Duggy"—Candice reached under the counter and then plonked a large pack of cards on the counter—"Card Combat III just released. Maybe you'd like to break in my store copy?"

Duggy looked uncertain for a moment then smiled and nodded.

"You okay, Duggy?" Candice asked. "You're a little subdued today."

Duggy looked at us frantically then turned back to Candice and gave a thumbs-up.

"He's got laryngitis," I offered. Laryngitis was a thing kids could get, right? "He's lost his voice. That's why he's so quiet."

Candice narrowed her eyes and stared at the little red line on Duggy's throat. She shrugged then reached under the counter again and pulled out a thick spiral notebook. It was labeled "Bestiary Rough Draft." "Okay, guys. You can play games here, but you need to hang out in the oubliette. I don't want you smelling up the place for other customers."

What the heck was an oubliette?

"BUT!" Candice flipped through her notebook. "You have to give me your opinion on some of the monsters I've been making for my bestiary." She flipped to the last page, made a few quick notes and doodles, closed it, and then held it out.

Tienna rolled her eyes, but Shane snatched the notebook and quick-stepped off to the rear of the store with a smile on his face. Candice went off to do comic-store owner stuff, and we piled into the oubliette, which turned out to be a spacious closet under a set of stairs.

Shane flipped through the spiral notebook. "This is so cool! I wish I could read faster. It's gonna take me forever to get through this."

We settled into ramshackle but oddly comfy folding chairs and breathed a sigh of relief.

"Are you okay, Duggy?" I asked.

Duggy nodded. He had a smile on his face.

"What happened?" I felt a little silly for asking something that wasn't a yes or no question. Duggy looked around for a moment then shrugged helplessly.

"Shane?" I asked. "Do you have a pen or pencil?"

"What? Yeah." Shane kept his nose buried in the bestiary and tossed a pen in my general direction. Shane always had a pen.

Tienna tore some sheets out of an old cleaning log and handed them to Duggy. He began scribbling furiously.

"These are so neat!" Shane had apparently forgotten about the awful worm that had kidnapped our friend.

"I like the teeth on that one," Tienna said grudgingly as she glanced over Shane's shoulder. I took a peek, too.

Everything in the book had very nasty teeth.

The door swung open. I jumped. Candice stepped in with a handful of chocolate bars and passed them out. We tore into them, except for Duggy. He kept scribbling.

"Do you like the bestiary so far, Shane?"

"Yeah!" Shane grinned. "But everything in here is so deadly. I'm afraid that the characters in my game would just die."

"I was actually hoping I could get your feedback on a new monster. Something special. Flip to the end."

I looked over Shane's shoulder as he turned to the last page. My eyes widened. All the other entries had been meticulously illustrated with dense text, but this one was only a few quick notes next to a loose sketch. We both recognized it.

Shane struggled to read. "Pro . . . mee . . . thee . . . an . . ."

"Worm," I said. "Promethean worm."

24 Unexpected Help

We all looked at each other.

Teddy, does she KNOW about it?!

Candice opened a chocolate bar and began listing the monster's traits. "About thirty feet long. Slimy. Tentacles sprouting from its head. Excellent camouflage skills. Photo phobic."

"What's photo phobic mean?" Tienna whispered without taking her eyes off Candice.

"Afraid of light," Shane replied.

Duggy poked my shoulder and thrust a piece of paper in front of my face.

MELISSA SAID THAT...
SO THEN I WENT TO THE FORT BECAUSE
IS GREAT AT HIDING AND HATES BRIGHT LIGHT BE
I THOUGHT IT WAS BECAUSE I HAD EGGS F
...IN A WHOLE MOOSE INTO TH
IT KEPT BRINGING SO

She totally knows about it!

"What else do you think we need to know about this thing?" Candice asked. "What would make it interesting?"

I half-raised my hand. "What does it want?" I asked.

Candice looked at me, very serious. "You ask good questions, Teddy."

"I was gonna ask that, too," Shane grumbled.

"Above all, it's curious. It loves to see new things. It travels to new places to experience strange and exotic plants and animals," said Candice.

"Well, that doesn't sound bad." Heather grinned nervously.

"And then it dissects them."

"Oh." Heather hugged her backpack.

"It's even been known to put things back together again, though it always seems to end up with a few parts left over."

Gross.

"And if it finds anything particularly interesting or useful, it takes a sample for later use."

"Later use?" Shane asked.

"Like a mad scientist," explained Candice. "It can take pieces of animals and plants and use them for its own purposes. It enjoys grafting these bits and pieces onto itself or using them in devices that it can grow to suit anything it needs."

An image of the worm's voice box flashed in my mind. I looked over at the little scar on Duggy's neck. He'd gone white as a sheet. I shivered.

"How do we kill it?" Tienna asked.

"I don't think you could." Candice looked a little worried. "It's freakishly strong, and I'm pretty sure it would have more than a few backup hearts floating around in its body."

"How do we get rid of it?" Heather kept hugging her backpack.

"Well, it's very secretive. If it thinks you know about it, it'll do its best to disappear. At the same time, though, it can be VERY protective of its samples."

We looked at Duggy.

Candice grinned. "That would be a good basis for an adventure, don't you think, Shane?"

"Yeah..." Shane replied. "Yeah, I guess..."

What does she mean by trouble, Teddy?!

Did she mean it wouldn't leave us alone?!

What if it takes Duggy back?

Oh no!

What if it comes for us next?

OH NO!

What if it does to Mr. Fuzzikins what it did to Duggy?

AGH!

My hands shook, and I nibbled at my pinky fingernail. Tienna reached over to pull my hand out of my mouth, but I stood and backed away from the table. My heart thumped. My breath came quicker and quicker. That awful feeling in the pit of my stomach crept toward my chest.

"Teddy, are you okay?" Heather asked.

"No... Yeah." I jammed my hands in my hoodie

pockets. "I need to pee."

"Bathroom's that way, Teddy." Candice pointed toward the front of the store.

I staggered into the bathroom and locked the door. I ran some water and splashed it on my face.

If you hadn't taken that picture, the worm would never have known about us, Teddy!

I know!

It's gonna come for you and your friends, Teddy!

I KNOW!

ALL of us are gonna wind up in those weird slimy bubbles and it's gonna be all . . . your . . . FAULT.

I sniffled.

There was a gentle knock at the door. "You okay, Teddy?" Candice asked.

I wiped my eyes with my shirt cuff and opened the door. "Yeah," I said. "I'm fine. I'm just worried is all."

Candice stared at me for a moment. I went to move past her, but she guided me back in front of her with an index finger.

"Your friends will forgive you for taking the picture, but they won't understand the real reason why you took it."

"What do you—"

Candice cut me off. "Shush, Teddy! I'm workin' here." She stared at me again then rolled her eyes. "I can't believe I have to say this, Teddy, but it's not gonna take your cat. Your cat will be perfectly safe."

Wait. How does she know that?

"But it's already taken something else," said Candice.

What?

"Something very important to you."

"WHAT?!"

"Teddy, SHUSH! The timing here is important."

WHAT THE HECK WAS HAPPENING RIGHT NOW?!

Candice rummaged in her pocket.

What the heck is going on, Teddy?!

"You've got a chance, Teddy. Slim, but it's still a chance." She took a deep breath and let it out slowly. "You need to remember a couple of things." Candice made her way back to the counter at the front of the store. I followed.

"You need to remember that your long slimy friend is, above all, curious. It wants to know EVERYTHING. You can talk to it if you appeal to its curiosity."

"Candice, how do you—"

"SHUSH, TEDDY!" Candice squeezed her eyes shut. "And you need to remember . . . Oh gosh darn it, what else did you need to remember?"

I held up the black marble. "Something about this?"

"Put that back in your pocket RIGHT NOW!"

Geez. Wrong line, apparently. I did as she said.

"Yes, something to do with that. When the time is right, you're going to squeeze that little marble three times, okay?"

"Candice, PLEASE just tell me—"

"And it will be up to you to know when that is, Teddy."

"But how... What..."

Candice grinned at me. "Just be yourself, Teddy, and everything will be fine." She looked off into the distance. "Well, MOSTLY fine, anyways."

The door to the shop opened with a polite DING. Martin strode in and smiled at me. He looked relieved.

Teddy!

Thanks for babysitting Milton after school. I really appreciate it.

Wait...

WHAT?!

"I should get him home, though. He gets cranky if he doesn't eat."

Milton

I ran back to the oubliette and dug Mr. Bear out of my backpack. Milton would NEVER have left Mr. Bear behind. I KNEW that.

Teddy, where's Milton?

"Oh no . . ." I whispered.

"Teddy, where's Milton?" Martin demanded.

Heather glanced up from reading Duggy's story.

"Mrs. Rose said that you picked him up after lunch."

"Well, I didn't!" Martin's voice cracked. He sounded a bit like me.

"Then who did?" Tienna asked.

"Oh no . . ." I whispered again. If it could disguise itself as Duggy, then maybe . . .

"What if it can look like anyone, not just Duggy?" Shane got it.

"Like who?" Heather asked.

"LIKE MARTIN!" I shouted.

Heather gasped.

Tienna swore loudly. "It's got him!"

"What's got him?!" Martin looked terrified.

"But we were just at its lair," Tienna pointed out. "We would've seen Milton."

"Maybe not," Shane replied. "We had to go digging for Duggy."

Martin's fingers pierced my arms like steel nails. Ow! "Teddy, WHO has him?"

"Not WHO, Martin." Shane grabbed Martin's shoulder. "WHAT."

"What?!" Martin looked close to tears. "Guys, I don't like this game!"

We all rushed to get our coats on.

"We have to go back to the fort!" Tienna said.

"Come with us, Martin." Heather pulled on Martin's sleeve. "We'll explain on the way."

"I don't want to come with you." Martin backed away. "I want my little brother!"

Everyone looked at a loss. How could we possibly prove to Martin that his little brother had been kidnapped by a slimy alien worm?

Wait . . . I had proof. I had proof in my pocket.

Don't do it, Teddy! Your friends will never forgive you! Tienna will KILL you!

You're right . . . They might not want to be my friends anymore. But Milton needs our help.

I took a deep breath, pulled out my dad's phone, and flipped to the picture of the worm.

"This," I said. "This is what took Milton."

Martin stared, dumbfounded.

We'd shown Martin the fort behind Duggy's house. Something had tried to collapse the tunnel, but it wasn't enough to keep us out. After Biscuit had made sure the worm wasn't down there, I'd taken Martin below. Even though many of the little spheres were gone, there were more than enough left to convince him that something awful and inhuman had once lived here. We hadn't found Milton.

Tienna, Shane, Duggy, and Heather had gone just a little ways down an unmarked trail to see if they could find a sign of the monster. Tienna shot withering glances back at me. She was still ticked that I'd taken a picture of the worm. I didn't blame her.

"No, Teddy, you don't get it." Martin looked up at me. He sniffled. I couldn't tell whether it was rain or tears on his face. "I SHOULD have believed you."

He totally should have! You're his cousin!

"Dad used to tell me all kinds of stories about things that live on the trails. Before . . . before he went missing."

"Uncle Toby went missing? My dad told me that he left."

Martin looked me square in the eye. "He went

MISSING, Teddy. Mom says that he left, but Dad would NEVER leave us. He used to walk the trails all the time. Lots of people go missing on the trails."

Oh geez. Wrong line, Teddy. "I'm sorry, Martin."

Martin sniffled. "It's okay."

"But if your dad just told you stories, why do you think you should have believed me?"

"Dad told me that one day I'd see that his tales were more than just ghost stories. He told me they'd be real. He TOLD me, Teddy. So I SHOULD have believed you . . . But I've just been so tired. Dad went missing, so Mom had to work more and more. Then Milton got sick last spring, and he had to be in the hospital. We had to go all the way down to Vancouver."

"Is that why he has hearing aids now?" I asked.

Martin nodded. "He got REALLY sick, Teddy. We were so scared. And I've been trying to help Mom, but she's run-down too. So when you told me that Duggy was a monster, I was just too tired and . . ." Martin bit at one of his fingernails. "And now my little brother's gone and we're never gonna find him! It's just gonna be me and Mom and she's gonna get even more depressed and then I'll turn into a troubled teen and take up smoking and I'll never see my little brother again!"

I guess I wasn't the only Meier who bit their nails and went down the anxiety rabbit hole. I sat beside Martin and put my hand on his shoulder. I knew that nothing I could say would make him feel better, but I had to try. "We'll find him, Martin."

I tried to hug him back as best I could (I'm not the best at hugging), and I was a little surprised when I told the truth. "I'm glad that I'm here, too."

No we aren't! This is a terrible, awful, nasty place and we can't wait to leave!

Shut up! Right now this isn't about us!

"Teddy! Martin!" Shane shouted from the trail they were checking out. "We found something!"

"Yes, come litter-cousins!" Biscuit shouted. "I have the scent, now. The tracks are fresh!"

Martin stared at me for a moment. "Did that hamster just talk?"

Right. Martin and Milton hadn't been around last week for the whole hamster thing. "It's a long story."

Forgiveness (Kinda)

We hurried over to where our friends stood on the path. It was one of five or six unmarked trails that crisscrossed through the woods. A curtain of rain and the sudden Ravensbarrow dusk kept us from seeing too far. I'd never stayed out this late. Mom and Dad weren't going to be happy with me. I really wished that my phone worked as a phone here.

"Biscuit says he can smell where the monster went." Heather snuggled the hamster. "Isn't that amazing?"

The hamster grinned, obviously enjoying Heather's affection. "The trail is fresh, young ape-pups. It reeks of cheese. But we must hurry! The rain shall wash away the scent if we are not quick upon our claws."

"You know, it probably would've still been here"—Tienna shot me an accusing glance—"but SOME-

BODY decided to scare it off!"

I shrank into my hoodie. "I'm sorry..."

"Sorry doesn't fix stupid, Teddy," Tienna stated.

"Okay, you need to get over it." Shane poked Tienna in the shoulder. "You always do this. You hold on to a grudge FOREVER. You need to move on."

"Move on?! Now BOTH Teddy and Duggy have almost gotten us killed. In a matter of days! Maybe they shouldn't even come with us."

Maybe we can just go home, Teddy!

No! We have to help Milton!

I want to help! Please! Duggy had grabbed a notebook and marker from his house. He scribbled furiously.

"No! How are we supposed to trust you, Duggy?"

"We all make mistakes, Tienna," Heather pointed out.

I'll make it up to you! Please. I'll do all the dangerous stuff. I'll go first, all the time. I'll be bait!

"Forgive or don't, ape-pups, but the trail grows cold," snarled Biscuit, perched on Heather's shoulder.

Tienna gritted her teeth. "FINE. You can be bait, Duggy."

She smiled and grabbed Duggy, putting him in a headlock. She noogied him roughly. "Besides. I kinda missed you."

She turned toward me. "And as for YOU, Teddy..."

Uh-oh...

"You got us into this mess, and you can help get us out of it."

Oh man. Was Tienna gonna forgive me? Just like that? RELIEF!

"BUT KNOW THIS," Tienna continued. "Someday, when you least expect it, I will carry out a dark, horrible vengeance of EPIC proportions. There will be a— What did you say I should call this, Shane?"

"A reckoning."

"There will be a day of reckoning, Teddy."

Gulp.

"Now let's go feed Duggy to a worm."

"Down the trail?" I asked. "An UNMARKED trail?"

"You're such a chicken, Teddy," said Tienna. She picked up a stick and swung it against a tree. She looked irritated when it broke. "Besides, I don't think we have a choice. Gremlin needs our help."

It's the one big rule, Teddy: NEVER go down an unmarked trail. It's gonna lead to a pit FILLED with those weird worm-monsters and they're gonna drink all your blood and spit your dried skin out to use as a rug!

I nibbled at one of my fingernails.

Is Milton worth it?

I took a deep breath then jammed my hands in my pockets.

"Tienna's right," I said. "We don't have a choice."

"Thanks, guys." Martin gave a little smile.

Tienna grabbed another stick and held it out like a sword. "Onward, then! To reclaim our gremlin!"

"I cannot believe you don't like D&D," Shane muttered.

"What's the stick for?" Heather asked.

"I'm not going worm hunting unarmed, Heather." Tienna swung her new stick and it also shattered against a tree. She swore. "Geez. I wish I had a sword or a mace or something."

Duggy perked up then went dashing back toward

his house. The sound of rustling foliage and Duggy's panting receded into the mist.

"Where the heck is Duggy going?" Shane asked.

I shrugged. "Maybe he has to pee."

A few moments later Duggy came back. Clutched in his arms was the old axe that had been buried in the stump in his backyard. He smiled and handed it to Tienna.

"Duggy, YES!" Tienna cackled and swung the axe experimentally. "You are now fully forgiven!"

The Ghost Bridge

We followed Biscuit as he darted along the trail. He was surprisingly quick considering his stubby little legs. More than a few times the trail would split or cross another trail, but Biscuit never hesitated. Without him we'd have been completely lost.

Probably forever, Teddy.

I started to overheat from all the running. I took off my raincoat even though it was raining so hard we might as well have been swimming. I noticed the others shedding layers, too, tucking them under bushes alongside the path. But Tienna and Martin were so athletic... I'd never seen either of them break a sweat. Was it getting warmer?

This was definitely a ghostly bridge. Oh geez . . . We were gonna cross it, and then it was gonna disappear stranding us on the other side! Forever! AGH!

"Okay, guys," Shane said. "What's the plan?"

"Find gremlin and rescue him," Tienna said matter-of-factly.

"But what if the worm decides to chase after us on the way back?" Shane asked. Good question, Shane. "I don't think we can outrun it."

"How big is it?" Martin asked. "Can we fight it?"

"Big!" Shane and Heather said together. Shane continued, "And no, we definitely can't fight it."

"Speak for yourself," Tienna snarled.

"What if we destroy the bridge after we cross it on the way back?" Shane asked. "You know, in case it's chasing us? It would slow the thing down at least."

"And how are we supposed to do that? Rig an elaborate system of ropes and pulleys? We don't know how much time we have," Tienna said.

Martin put his hand on Shane's shoulder. "It's a good idea, but we need to keep moving."

Biscuit scurried up onto the bridge railing. "I can be of assistance." He clasped his little hamster paws at Heather, pleading.

"Um . . . We kind of need you to show us the way, Biscuit. But thank you."

"You misunderstand, my queen!" Biscuit cupped his paws around his mouth and let loose a squeaky hamster howl out into the mist behind us.

FOR THE GLORY OF HEATHER!

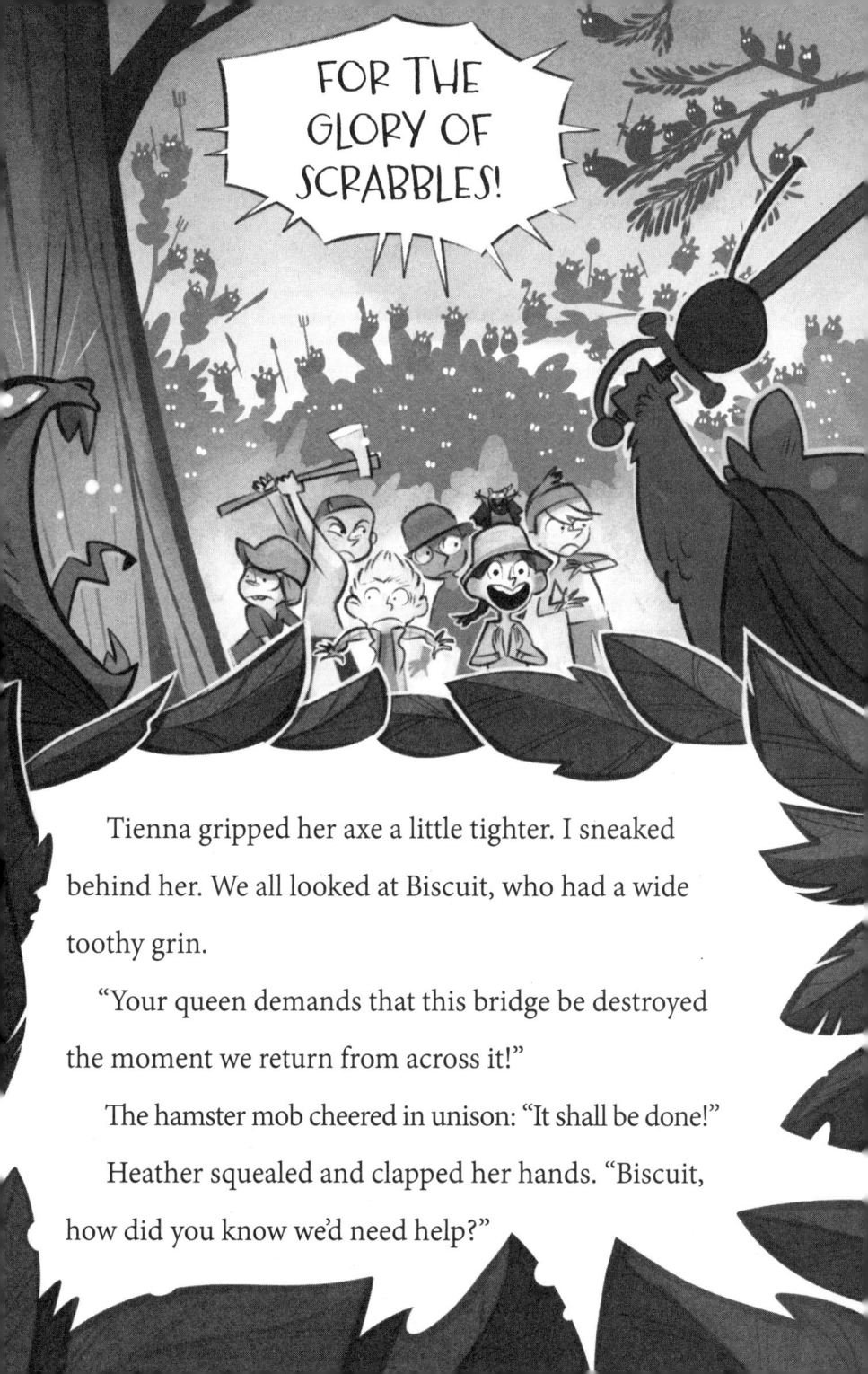

Tienna gripped her axe a little tighter. I sneaked behind her. We all looked at Biscuit, who had a wide toothy grin.

"Your queen demands that this bridge be destroyed the moment we return from across it!"

The hamster mob cheered in unison: "It shall be done!"

Heather squealed and clapped her hands. "Biscuit, how did you know we'd need help?"

Several of the hamster army shouted from the forest. "You are guarded day and night, my queen. We are always here! Always!"

"But there is one problem, my queen." Biscuit turned to Heather. He flattened his ears and looked as piteous as possible. I'd never seen a hamster's eyes get that large and sparkly before. "They require a firm hand in leadership."

We watched as the many hamsters nibbled experimentally at the bridge ropes.

"Stay here and lead," Biscuit implored. "I shall accompany your comrades and guide them truthfully." The hamsters cried out, joining his plea. Hundreds of little hamster paws clasped, begging.

Heather turned toward us apologetically. "They really do need me, guys." She picked up one of her hamster minions. The other hamsters looked on, jealous that they hadn't been chosen. "They can't do much without being told."

"I don't like this!" Tienna gripped her axe with white knuckles. "What's to keep you from leading us off the path, rat?"

"I swear on the life of my queen." Biscuit stood bolt upright, placed one paw over his heart, and waved at Martin with the other. "I shall guide you to this filthy ape-pup's litter-mate."

It would be a really REALLY good idea to make it so that the worm-thing couldn't follow us back home.

Trust a hamster?! They're gonna eat us, Teddy!

We have to help Milton!

"We need to go, Tienna," I said, "and I trust Biscuit."

Duggy tugged on my shirt. He shot a nervous glance at Biscuit then turned to me and shook his head.

"Don't worry, Duggy," I said. "Biscuit's been a great help. Besides, we're Heather's friends. I don't think he'd let anything happen to us."

Duggy looked uncertain.

"The trail runs cold, foe of Scrufflechops! Make your choice!"

Tienna growled, obviously fighting a deep and growing urge to start swatting hamsters with her axe, then she marched across the bridge. Duggy dashed after her.

"Onward then, ape-pups!"

Ravensbarrow?

The bridge turned out to be pretty sturdy, and we almost didn't need Biscuit. The path, though winding, was the only one through the forest.

The rain had eased up but was replaced by an awful muggy wetness. Everything smelled rotten. But not rotting leaves rotten. Rotten like cheese. The trees became twisted and misshapen. They shot up so high we couldn't see the tops through the mist. Bright flowers grew out of every little space that wasn't the slimy path.

It was actually really pretty.

"I didn't know Ravensbarrow had flowers like these," I said.

"It doesn't," Shane said.

"But it does, Shane. Look!" I pointed at a large, vibrant blue flower with petals as big as my hand.

Teddy . . .

I don't think this is Ravensbarrow anymore.

We hadn't gone far from the bridge when the trail opened out into a barren clearing. The rain stopped like someone had turned off the faucet, and the mist cleared instantly. A mud hut bigger than my house was surrounded by a tangle of fallen trees with gnarled, snaking branches. Compared to the living forest we'd just run through, this place was completely dead. Sterile, even. A single pink light shone through one of the hut's windows. Up above we could see a clear sky and some twinkling stars.

The sky was purple. A vibrant, deep purple.

WHERE WERE WE?!

"Mrs. Sergeant told me some pretty weird ghost stories but never anything like this," Tienna whispered.

"My dad did." Martin took a deep breath and picked his way toward the mud hut. Tienna, Shane, and Duggy followed him.

Something with too many teeth and with eyes in the wrong place flew overhead in the deep-purple sky. It smiled at me.

AGH!

Teddy, I wanna go home!

We can't.

Teddy, PLEASE! I wanna go home!

We CAN'T.

Not without Milton.

I clenched my fists to keep my fingers out of my mouth and followed my friends.

So Many Squirrels!

The mud hut reeked of cheese.

Slimy bubbles of every size were glued to the many snaking pillars that stretched from floor to ceiling. Each one had an animal or plant inside. I glanced into them as we snuck deeper into the worm-thing's lair.

Squirrels

Flowers

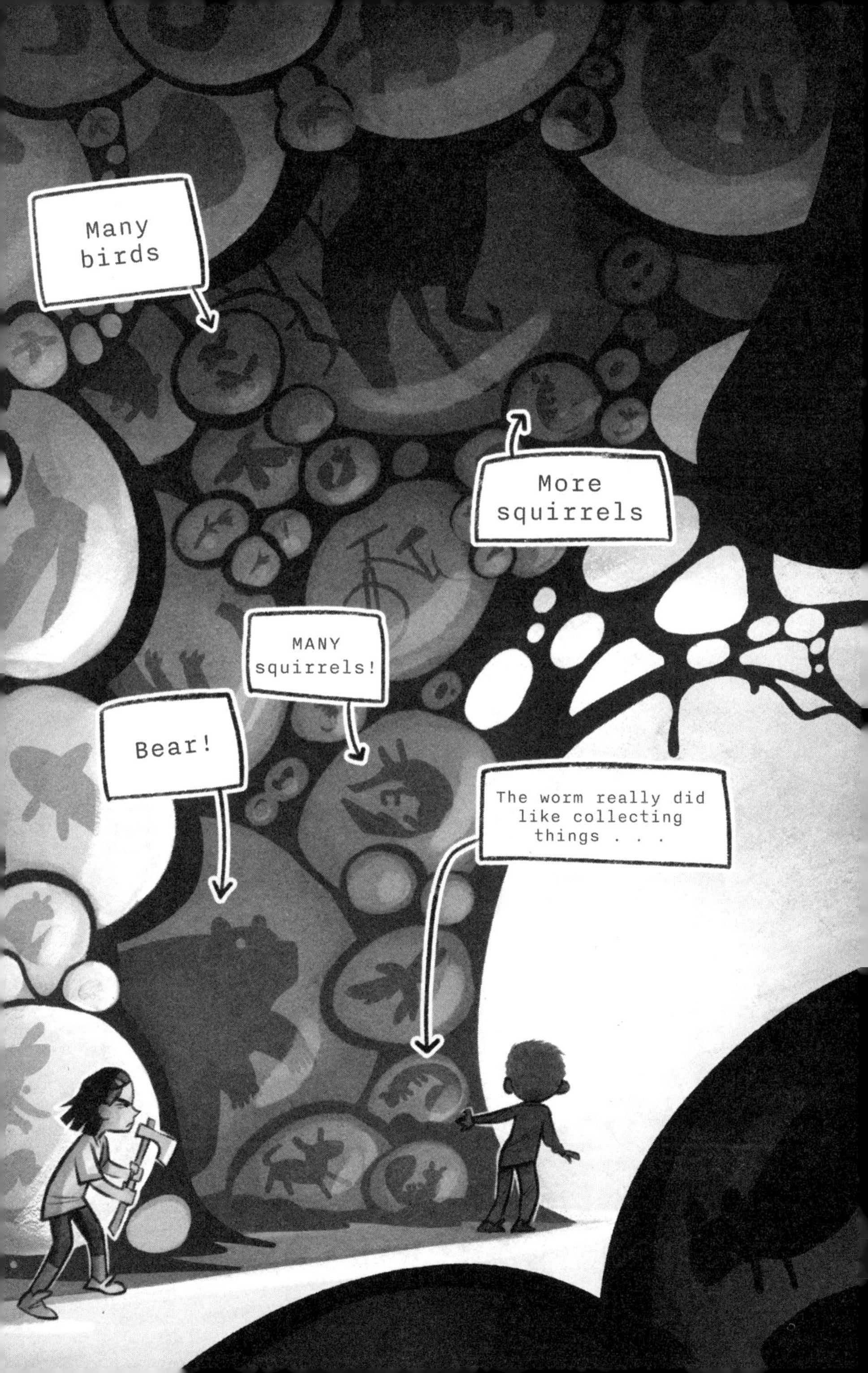

Many birds

More squirrels

MANY squirrels!

Bear!

The worm really did like collecting things . . .

Duggy went first, just like he'd promised. We snuck between the bubble pillars toward the center of the hut then hid behind a massive bubble that contained a moose (a MOOSE?!). Duggy peeked around it then ducked back to us and mimed awful flailing tentacles. Carefully, we poked our heads around the side of the bubble.

Thousands of bugs glowed the same eerie deep purple as the sky outside, bathing the room in soft evil light. The worm was coiled behind a wide slab of raised dirt, and it was slathering slime over a green, liquid-filled sphere. Inside was a little figure in an oversized coat and a hat with little bear ears.

Milton.

"If we can get across this gap, we can sneak all the way around to him." Tienna nodded at the open space between us and the next pillar of bubbles.

"But how do we get the worm away from Milton?" I asked.

"One of us could create a distraction," Shane suggested.

Duggy perked up and pointed to himself. He mouthed the word "bait." He scribbled in his notebook. **I'm very distracting!**

Shane shook his head. "No, Duggy. You're not distracting, you're distractABLE."

Duggy frowned mutinously. He flipped through his notebook to an older page and tapped it with his marker.

I'll make it up to you! Please. I'll do all the dangerous stuff. I'll go first, all the time. I'll be bait!

"No, Duggy." Tienna patted Duggy on the shoulder. "I'll distract it. I'm the best runner." Duggy frowned again then peeked back around the moose bubble at the worm.

Martin put his hand on Tienna's shoulder. "Thank you, Tienna."

She tightened the laces on her shoes. "All of you sneak across the gap. Once you're on the other side, I'll get the worm's attention."

I looked at the space that stretched before us between the bubble pillars. If someone ran at the wrong time the worm would easily spot them. "Who's gonna go first?" I whispered.

The worm turned its head and Duggy sprang to his feet and dashed across the gap.

Tienna flapped her mouth open and closed as if swearing intensely and waved her arms in a way that meant "What the heck are you doing?!"

Duggy peeked around his pillar. He had a much better view from where he was. He tapped his notebook again then held up his hand to say "Stop!"

The beast leaned below the table. Duggy's eyes went wide, and he frantically motioned us toward him. Martin ran in a low crouch and settled in behind Duggy.

Tienna gritted her teeth in resignation, and when Duggy and Martin motioned to us, she pushed Shane out to send him across the gap.

Tienna held me by the shoulders. "Ready, Teddy?"

"Ready," I whispered back.

Tienna gave me a weird look. "You know, Teddy, you're a lot more calm and collected than you were with the hamsters."

I guess I wasn't showing it, but I was absolutely terrified. My hands were clenched (to keep my fingers out of my mouth) so hard they were shaking. My knees were weak. I wouldn't have been able to move without Tienna's help. "I'm not leaving my little cousin behind." Tienna smiled grimly.

"Ready, Biscuit?" I asked.

Biscuit grinned from his perch on my shoulder. "Ready."

Duggy, Martin, and Shane waved at us. Tienna pushed me out into the open. I didn't get far.

I jumped at the sudden noise and tripped, coming to a skidding halt on my hands and knees.

The worm whipped its head up and fixed its many eyes on me.

Tienna ran out of hiding and tried to pull me up, but it was too late. We'd been spotted.

Biscuit hissed in my ear. "For the glory of Scrabbles, Pukey Bear, you must PAY for your transgressions."

The thing moved toward us, slithering with its snaky bits and pulling itself across the ground with its hands.

Tienna gripped her axe and snarled.

"DIE!"

31
The Marble

Biscuit leaped off my shoulder and scuttled away into the maze of alien slime spheres.

The axe clattered to the ground. Tienna stopped moving.

I managed to get to my feet and glanced to my right. Martin, Shane, and Duggy were nowhere to be seen.

They'd left me.

They left us!

But they were gonna help Milton.

But they LEFT us, Teddy!

They'll come back!

WILL they?!

YES!

But I was the bait now whether I liked it or not.

The thing reared up to its full height and fixed all three of its eyes on me. A hand gracefully moved to the bone box hanging around its neck. Simultaneously, it worked the crank and swept its monstrous fingers across the holes on the box's surface.

"I suppose I can always use more spare parts. Your spleens are magnificent little organs." Duggy's voice echoed from the box.

What had Candice said? It liked to talk? It was curious? Oh geez. What should I say here? What could I possibly say to this thing?!

The other hand shot out, grabbed me by my shirt, and lifted me off the ground.

The worm was silent and still for what seemed like forever. "Yes. Yes, I would very much like to know this. Also how. I was unaware you little things could walk the trails."

Just beyond the monster I saw Martin creeping toward Milton's sphere. They didn't leave me! Now I had to give Martin time to get to Milton . . .

"I could see you back at my school. Me and Tienna followed you because we . . . we were curious."

"You could see me, too?" A deep throaty rumbling echoed from the worm's breathing holes. "Today is a good day. Only one other organism has been able to see through my sonic camouflage." An eyeball on a stalk hovered inches from my face. "Three specimens are better than one."

Uh-oh.

"What do you mean by specimens?" I asked.

You HAD to ask, Teddy.

"For dissection."

UH-OH.

"You possess a very special sense that I am eager to learn more about." The worm coiled back into place. Its tail continued to wiggle. "My sonic disguise, though effective against all other naked wandering apes, is of no use against you. I must discover why."

IT'S GONNA STEAL OUR EYES, TEDDY!

"Won't... won't that hurt?" I stammered.

"Unlikely. Your nervous system is not complicated."

I glanced behind the worm again. Martin had reached Milton's bubble! Shane and Duggy were with him, too. I had to buy them enough time to break Milton free. Oh man, and then we had to get Tienna back...

One thing at a time, Teddy!

I felt Milton's hearing aid in my pocket next to my phone. The worm thought we could see it because of something natural. What if I showed it the truth? Maybe the hearing aid would be enough to keep the worm occupied... Or maybe I could use the flash on my phone...

"What if I told you that I could see you with a device?

What if I could show you?" I fiddled for the phone.

"Go on..."

"If I show you, will you let my little cousin go?"

"Perhaps..." The taloned hand squeezed. "But I saw the light-device you used in my storehouse. If I see it again, I will remove your hands."

Well, okay then.

I pulled the hearing aid out instead. "Milton could see you using one of these. It's a device that amplifies sound. He has a hard time hearing people, so he needs help."

The worm plucked the hearing aid from my hand. Three of the eyes investigated it while the other four continued intense observations of my own eyeballs.

"Primitive." The worm crushed the hearing aid into little bits. "You are obviously lying. Such a random collection of minerals and processed petroleum cannot do the things you say it can."

The worm turned and began moving back toward its table, taking me along for the ride. I saw Martin duck behind the slab. Shane and Duggy were hidden among the bubbles.

"Waitwaitwait!" I cried. "You're right, I was lying!"

"Primitive."

Oh my gosh. Nonononono . . . It was gonna cut me open and haul out my wiggly innards and there was-nothingIcoulddotostopit! AGH!

I scrabbled in my pocket again. I had to use my phone and hope that the worm was too slow to tear off my hands before I flashed it.

That's not a good plan, Teddy!

But instead of my phone, Candice's little marble settled into my hand. Was now the right time to use it?

"I'll tell you the truth!" I gripped the marble. "I didn't want you to have the real thing that lets us see you."

The worm stopped dead. All seven eyes hovered inches from my face. "Show me. NOW."

Yup. This seemed like the right time.

I held the marble out.

"I can see you with this."

I squeezed the marble three times.

SCRAAAW!

The marble flashed over and over again, filling the dim mud hut with bright strobing light. The worm's scream rattled my skull. It reared back and covered its eyes, dropping me to the ground. Its long snaky body coiled and writhed with each eye-melting blast of light. The needle-toothed mouth opened, dripping cheesy slime. It wasn't smart, or curious, anymore.

It was ENRAGED.

The mouth opened wider.

My knees quivered. My feet were glued to the ground.

Duggy leapt out of his hiding spot among the many bubbles. He scooped up the axe and chopped at Tienna's prison.

She slid out onto the floor and gasped for air. She was on her feet in a split second.

The mouth opened WIDER.

"KEEP FLASHING, TEDDY!" Tienna bellowed. She snatched the axe out of Duggy's hands.

I held the marble above my head. The worm reared back, screeching. Cheesy slime sprayed everywhere.

Tienna ran at the worm with her axe. Martin had busted Milton's bubble and was dragging his surprised little brother out of the mud hut as fast as he could.

"Tienna, no!" Shane yelled. "It's too big!"

"Trust me, Shane!" She ran toward the worm but at the last second veered to her right and brought her axe down on the largest bubble in the room.

The moose wasted no time going on a stompy rampage, charging in random directions and smashing through specimen bubbles like they were tissue paper. Animals of every shape and size—and a SWARM of confused, desperate squirrels—flooded the mud hut.

A shocked deer slammed into me, and I dropped the flashing marble. I ran after it, but Tienna grabbed me and threw me toward the exit.

"Run, Teddy! Leave it!"

We dashed out into the clear purpled air along with a few hundred animals that fled into the alien forest. I saw Martin and Milton running back along the path toward the bridge. Tienna and I emerged with Shane and Duggy.

Oh my gosh, we were outside.

WE'D DONE IT!

The flashing light stopped. Another skull-shattering shriek rang out from the mud hut.

"GO!" Tienna shoved us forward. "We gotta get back to the bridge!"

We sprinted along the winding path. As we got nearer to the bridge, I heard the snapping of tree limbs and crashing of branches behind us. My skull vibrated as the alien shriek got closer and closer.

It was following us!

We popped out of the forest and saw Heather, Martin, and Milton on the other side of the bridge. The bridge was still there! It wasn't a ghost bridge! RELIEF!

"Teddy!" Milton jumped up and down. "Over here, Teddy!"

"Come on!" Martin shouted.

Heather's eyes went wide, and she pointed behind us. The worm crashed out of the forest and lashed out a hand toward me.

Tienna chopped at the hand with her axe, leaving a nasty slice, and the worm recoiled.

"CUT THE BRIDGE!" I heard a familiar squeak. Biscuit! I was gonna kick him so hard that his tail was gonna shoot through his—

Teddy, I agree, but tangent!

"NO!" Heather yelled. "They're not across yet!"

Tienna shoved Shane and me forward, and the three of us dashed onto the bridge. The ropes groaned and the boards swayed from side to side as we scrambled over them. We were almost all the way over when the whole bridge lurched under our feet. The worm, which probably weighed as much as a car, stretched the ropes to their breaking point as it slithered after us.

"Cut it!" Biscuit shrieked. "CUT IT NOW!"

"No, Biscuit!" Heather yelled.

I fell to the bridge deck, but Martin and Milton grabbed my arms and pulled me up. Shane sprinted alongside me, and we made it across the bridge. Tienna leapt, clawing at the dirt.

"NOW!" Heather bellowed.

The bridge fell away. We didn't hear it hit the ground. How deep WAS the ravine?!

The misty forest was silent.

We sat there for a moment and just breathed. I lay back and closed my eyes. We were across. We were alive. We were safe!

Martin hugged his little brother.

We'd done it!

We all laughed. Milton hugged me.

But then . . .

I Get a Terrible Idea

"Please, calm down! We just wanted our friend back!" Shane pleaded with the worm as he got to his feet and backed away from the edge of the ravine.

But the worm wouldn't listen. The intelligent, curious thing back in the mud hut had been replaced by a predatory beast.

It REALLY didn't like flashing lights.

"For the queen!" Hamsters leapt forward and jabbed the worm with kitchen knives and forks. It didn't even notice. A hand whipped out, grabbed Shane by his ankles, and lifted him into the air. The mouth opened wide.

Oh no . . . Someone was gonna get eaten!

Tienna ran forward with her axe, but the worm's other hand knocked her into the forest.

The mouth opened wide enough to swallow us all.

Someone was definitely gonna get eaten!

Martin tried to push his little brother out of the way, but the worm's free hand grabbed Milton by his hood and lifted him up.

Milton!

Someone was gonna get eaten
unless I did something!

The worm fell to the ground and shrieked at me. The tips of its tentacles split open revealing little slime-spitting mouths.

AGH!

FLASH!

Every flash made it pause in pain. After a second it charged, using its arms to drag itself just a little bit faster and shedding its coat of hamsters.

My lizard brain kicked in. I ran, screaming, back toward Ravensbarrow (I hoped). The worm shrieked as it slithered after me. At least if it was chasing me, it wasn't eating my friends. I pointed my phone over my shoulder and kept pressing the photo button. Flashes of light and horrid alien screeches reverberated through the misty trees.

The path split ahead of me, so I cut to the right and hid behind a fallen tree on the side of the path. The worm raced by scattering leaves and uprooting small trees, sounding like a cement slab being dragged through the forest.

It hadn't seen me! Phew.

But I had no idea which way to go. Biscuit had led us in,

and I hadn't paid attention. I sat, panting and whimpering, in a nest of soggy leaves. "What do I do now?" I whispered. I sniffled, and a couple of tears dropped to the leafy ground. (Yes, I cried again. I cry when I'm really scared, okay?)

I hung my head then gasped. I was crying on a glowing purple mushroom. In fact, the whole trail was lined with luminescent mushrooms. Candice HAD mentioned that her shortcut would be easier to see at night... She'd been right about the marble, so maybe I could trust her on this, too. It's not like I had many other options... I scrambled up and ran as quietly as I could along it.

I heard the worm somewhere in the forest. Never in sight because of the chilly mist but always there. I could smell it, too. It was still trying to find me.

Without warning, the forest opened up, and I tripped over a stretch of railroad. I fell onto the rough gravel under the rails. Ow. Stretching in front of me, I saw a maze of train cars, shacks, and crates. The air here was cold. I'd left my coat back in the forest. I shivered, but it was only partly because of the chill.

The train yard.

Wait a minute... The train yard was on the other side of Ravensbarrow. How the heck had I circled around the entire town without crossing a road or a river? How had I missed the lake? It wasn't possible, but Candice was right!

Wonderful! Now we can choose between getting eaten by a giant dog or an alien worm.

THAT'S NOT A GOOD CHOICE, TEDDY!

I heard the worm's telltale slimy dragging and looked behind me. The trees quivered as it forced its way toward me. I smelled its slime.

It smelled cheesy.

Why did everything in this foul, wet, HORRIBLE place have to revolve around dairy?! Why couldn't it have been CINNAMON or something? I could've handled ANYTHING else, but no. It's always MILK. Or CHEESE.

Wait. Martin had said some-

thing about cheese... "All dogs love cheese, Teddy."

Oh man. I had an idea.

No, Teddy!

A terrible idea.

A TERRIBLE idea, Teddy!

The worm screeched. Though I still couldn't see it, my eyeballs vibrated in my skull. The stench of ancient cheese washed over me.

I took a deep breath, stumbled down the gravel slope, and ran into the train yard.

BIG DOG!

My feet crunched on the gravel. My knuckles were white from gripping my phone. I moved around the puddles that looked suspiciously like colossal paw prints and leaned against a train car to catch my breath. I had NEVER run that much before in my life.

Huff... Pant... Gasp...

How the heck was I supposed to get the dog's attention?

We can just keep running, Teddy. We can go home.

Huff. Gasp. Pant.

I'm not bringing an enraged alien monster back to Mom and Dad!

Mom could handle it. She can handle anything.

Gasp. Huff. Phew.

I'm not bringing an enraged alien monster back to Mr. Fuzzikins!

Okay, fair point.

I stopped panting. I'd finally caught my breath, but my heart still felt like it wanted to escape through my throat.

Pant. Pant. Pant.

Wait a minute . . . I wasn't panting anymore.

PANT...

PANT...

PANT...

Hot, rotten breath washed over me from above. A deep growl shook the train car.

"I told you what would happen if you came back," the dog rumbled.

I froze just like the last time I'd seen the dog. My legs quivered. My lips moved, but I could only whimper.

The dog leaned down, snatched me by my shirt in its twisted fangs, and lifted me into the air.

AGH!

It's gonna eat us, Teddy!

AAAAAAARGH!

The long tongue licked my head, leaving a long tail of drool dripping to the ground. I'm certain I saw a coyote skull stuck between the dog's teeth. AGH!

"I hear humans taste like pork chops," the dog growled.

SAY SOMETHING, TEDDY!

"Wa . . . wait!" I stuttered. "I hear you like cheese!" I still had my phone clutched in my hand.

"Boy-bacon will have to do," the dog chuckled.

"Huge cheese!" I pleaded. "Colossal cheese!" I struggled for more words meaning "big." Mr. Spinnaker loved big words and used them all the time! WHY DID I NEVER PAY ATTENTION IN CLASS?!

Titanic, Teddy! Titanic!

"Titanic cheese!" I yelled. I opened the camera app on my phone as I hung from the hound's teeth.

"I see no wheel of cheddar in your pockets, boy!"

"It'll be here in a second!" I pointed my camera down into the misty train yard and took a picture. Flash! The worm screeched close by!

"You DARE take a picture of me?!"

I snapped another picture. FLASH! The worm screeched, closer.

The dog whipped its head side to side, shaking me like a chew toy. My shirt ripped, and my phone flew out of my hands, landing in one of the many paw-print puddles below.

My pictures!

"I'm going to eat you feet first for that," the dog

barked, shaking the rail cars. It tossed me into the air, just like it had done with that poor coyote.

"You may not have room after the cheese plate!" I yelled in my most awesome, confident voice.

Teddy, that's not what happened.

I braced stoically for what was going to come next?

Nope.

I squealed and made myself into a little ball. I think I peed my pants.

Yup.

I fell toward the open mouth and lolling tongue, but just before the hound's jaws snapped shut, the worm slithered up the dog's giant furry leg toward me. The worm was STILL trying to eat me first!

The dog barked in surprise and reared back. I bounced off its furry chest and fell into the same giant paw-print puddle where my phone lay.

The hound fell backward and knocked a train car off the rails. I stumbled away as fast as I could amid a cacophony of squealing steel, surprised snarling barks, and screeching alien howls. The two monsters rolled away across the train yard, fighting desperately. I wasn't sure who to bet on!

A hand grabbed me by the shoulder. AGH! But it was just Tienna. Oh my gosh, it was Tienna! She hustled me toward one of the many stacks of cargo containers that littered the train yard. Martin, Milton, Shane, Heather, and Duggy huddled there, watching the fight between the dog and the worm.

The dog grabbed the worm by the tail, whipped it into the air, and snapped its jaws shut with a slimy SQUELCH. It chewed several times, but its teeth just seemed to bounce off the worm's alien hide.

"You were right, Martin!" I laughed, though I was still absolutely terrified. "All dogs like cheese!"

"I told you, Martin—big dog!" Milton pointed and grinned his I-told-you-so grin.

"Teddy, that's NOT the dog I was talking about." Martin's voice cracked and he hugged his little brother.

"Yeah, I KNOW!" I leaned against the cargo container. My heart pumped so fast it could have drained the lake. "Maybe believe us next time!"

The dog, realizing that chewing wasn't going to work, threw back its head. It horked the worm down whole, swallowing it with one final resounding GULP.

"Guys, we need to leave," said Tienna, picking me up by my torn shirt.

"Y-yeah," Shane stuttered. "Let's go."

None of us had taken our eyes off the dog. It turned toward us. Glowing blue eyes flashed wide and wild. Foamy drool glooped from its slime-stained lips. Blood leaked from several nasty-looking bites inflicted by the worm.

"YOU!" The bark was so loud I thought my eardrums would burst. Before we could even stand, it had cleared half the train yard and was bearing down on us.

Milton screamed. Martin threw his little brother over a shoulder and ran. Duggy and Shane helped me to my feet and Tienna readied her axe. Heather froze.

GURGLE.

Suddenly the dog stopped, a confused look on its face. I could see its stomach churning. I could see something IN its stomach wriggling.

HURK!

The dog's tongue lolled as it gagged, and then . . .

A swimming pool of cheesy slime, whatever else the dog had eaten (not us, thankfully!), and the flailing worm schlorped to the ground. With a hiss and scrunching of gravel the worm slithered back toward the forest.

The dog kept puking.

We ran.

We didn't stop until we'd reached downtown Ravensbarrow. I finally collapsed on the sidewalk outside the Nerd's Roost. We gasped and huffed to catch our breath (even Tienna). One by one we looked at each other. Milton started to laugh. Martin hugged his little brother and started to chuckle as well. Tienna guffawed and punched Shane in the arm before grabbing Duggy and giving him a vicious noogie. Heather let loose a huge sigh of relief. I started to giggle. We weren't dead. Ha! Hilarious!

Off in the distance we heard a howl. Two blue eyes glared at us from the misty train yard.

We ducked into the comic shop.

35
Board Games

"I know." Shane said. "Sorry about that."

Candice had given each of us a chocolate bar and sat us down in the oubliette again. We were all dirty, scraped, bruised, and covered in alien cheese slime. She'd given me a shirt to replace my torn one.

She grinned. "It's okay. I was kind of expecting it this time. Do you have any details for my bestiary?"

"It doesn't like getting hit with an axe." Tienna grinned as she munched her chocolate bar.

"I'm surprised! You're stronger than you look." Candice chuckled. "Well, tonight's a busy night, so here's a phone. You should probably call your parents to pick you up." She tossed the store's phone on the table and left the room. I scooted out of my seat and caught up to her in the hallway. I had so many questions.

"Candice, wait! We crossed a bridge in the woods and then we were somewhere completely different. Where were we?"

She shrugged. "The woods?"

"What? No." I shook my head. Candice didn't get

it. "The sky was purple, Candice. We were somewhere ELSE. Like, really, really else."

She cocked an eyebrow. "Deep in the woods?"

I tried a different question. "Well, does the worm come back? Do we have to worry about it anymore?"

"How would I know that, Teddy?"

"Well . . . Milton said that you're from the future."

Candice snort-chuckled. "Of course I'm not. Don't be silly. But I don't think you have anything to worry about. If you were eaten alive by a giant dog then thrown up, would you want to stick around?"

"Well . . . no. Wait, how did you know about that?!"

Candice patted me on the shoulder. "I told you already, Teddy, everything's gonna turn out okay." She walked a little ways down the hall then turned back to me and shrugged. "Well . . . mostly okay."

There was a tournament of some kind tonight and the back of the store was packed with people playing card games. The store was warm and bright, and the laughter of people having fun made me feel safe. I joined everyone in the oubliette. We ate our chocolate bars in silence for a few moments.

Tienna slammed her fist on the table. "WHAT WAS UP WITH THAT DOG?!"

"Where WERE we?" Shane cut in.

"And what happened to the hamsters?" I asked.

"Civil war," Shane replied.

"It was awful, Teddy." Heather looked distraught. "As soon as the worm chased after you, Biscuit told the rest of the guard to attack Shane, Duggy, and Tienna. I told them to come with me and help, and then they all started fighting."

"It was wild!" Tienna waved her arms. Duggy nodded in agreement and waved his arms, too. "Half of them screamed 'FOR THE QUEEN!' while Biscuit and the rest yelled 'FOR SCRABBLES!' and then they got into a huge fuzzy fight!"

"It was straight out of *The Lord of the Rings*," Shane added.

"We left them back in the woods so we could chase after you," Martin said. He gave Milton the rest of his chocolate bar.

There was another moment of silence.

Milton gobbled down his chocolate bar.

Duggy nudged Tienna and pointed at the phone. He held his hand up to his ear and mimed talking into it. It took us a moment to remember that Duggy couldn't talk. I couldn't help but stare at the thin red line on his neck.

Tienna looked like she was about to cry but nodded. Duggy dialed a number and Tienna picked up the phone. She moved away from the table to check if Duggy's parents were home.

"Duggy, what happened?" Shane asked.

Duggy looked helpless.

"I think . . . I think it put part of Duggy in the box it was using to talk," I said. Duggy nodded.

"Did it hurt?" Martin whispered.

Duggy shook his head and then smiled. He seemed happy to be back with us, but was he ever gonna talk again?

Tienna came back to the table. "They're on their way, Duggy. They were worried that you weren't at home, but they didn't sound angry." She sat back down beside Duggy. "I didn't know what to say about your voice..."

Duggy shrugged and smiled at her. Tienna leaned over and gave him a huge hug.

I'm still angry at you, Duggy.

But I'm never letting you out of my sight again.

One by one we phoned our parents. Dad sounded relieved then disappointed. I'd never stayed out this late before. He said we'd have to talk about it. Aw, man...

"Did you get any good pictures, Teddy?" Shane asked. "We had some really good angles!"

My phone! Well, my dad's phone. Man, he wasn't

gonna be happy about how I left it in a puddle in the train yard. "No, my phone's gone. No pictures."

Oh my gosh, this whole time I'd been worried about pictures. One of my best friends had been MISSING, and I'd still been worried about getting PICTURES!

We were about to waltz out of the worm's lair with everyone safe and sound, and instead of sneaking away, I took a PICTURE. And then it turned out the worm had kidnapped my little cousin. My friends and family had been in danger this entire time and it had all been because . . . of . . . ME!

I flopped my head to the table and wept.

"Hey, it's okay, Teddy." Shane patted me on the shoulder. "We can get you a new camera."

"It's not that," I sniffled. "This is all my fault."

"What do you mean, Teddy?" Heather looked concerned as she nibbled her chocolate bar.

"All this happened because I wanted to go looking for weird things. Because I wanted pictures of weird stuff. Because . . . because . . ."

"Tienna!" Shane grabbed at Tienna. "What the heck are you doing?!"

"Look at him," Tienna snarled. "He's trying to blame himself!" She slammed the table with a fist. "Teddy, you are NOT to blame for any of this—none of it, hear me?"

"But I . . . I . . ?" I wanted to leave them . . . GUILT!

"Teddy, I'm the one who suggested that we look for other paranormal things, not you," Shane said. "Besides, Duggy and Milton would have been kidnapped whether or not we wanted to look for weird things."

Duggy nodded.

"Actually, Teddy," Heather chimed in, "if you weren't looking for things like the worm, we may not have noticed."

"And if we hadn't looked for weird things around Ravensbarrow, you never would have run into the train yard dog," Shane added.

"And we never would've been able to find Milton." Martin clapped me on the shoulder.

"Though taking that picture was pretty dumb," Tienna pointed out. "So I guess you're a LITTLE to blame for this."

"But we've forgiven you, Teddy!" Shane stared at Tienna meaningfully as he moved off to the board game shelf. "And even though this was a weird, messed-up night, NO ONE IS TO BLAME. So... who's up for a game of Zombie Splat?"

"I wanna be red!" Milton shouted.

Tienna smoothed out my shirt. "Come play board games with us, Teddy."

Shane set up the board game. I watched my friends laugh as they started rolling dice and moving pieces around. I had a belly full of chocolate (my parents NEVER let me have chocolate), and the comic store was warm and bright. The rain pattered on the roof. It felt like this room with my friends was the only place in the world.

If all of Ravensbarrow were like this, I might get used to it. Yeah. I could get used to this. If I kept my head down maybe I could leave all the dangerous spooky stuff around here alone.

Everything was gonna be okay.

Home

"MOMMY!" Milton tore through my front door and tackled his mother.

"Baby boo! We were getting worried..." Auntie Morgan sniffed a couple of times.

Oh my gosh! Milton, you smell like a sewer!

What the heck happened to you three?!

"Hi Mom." Martin gave a little wave and smiled apologetically.

"I was kidnapped by a giant monster with too many teeth and it was gonna peel me open to steal my organs!" Milton cackled.

My dad walked in and closed the door behind us. "Well, make sure the monster knows you have to be home before dark next time." He chuckled. "First hamsters, and now organ-stealing monsters. Sounds like fun!"

"Not really," said Martin.

"No?" Dad asked.

"OF COURSE NOT, DAD!" I said. "What part of that sounds fun? It was gonna dissect us alive!"

My mom poked her head in from the kitchen. "Technically that's called vivisection, Teddy. Which I'll do the next time you don't call to let us know where you are."

"Gross," I replied. I was pretty sure Mom was joking.

Mom took a look at me and Martin. She wrinkled her nose. "YOU'RE gross. And I'm not joking, Teddy." She hurried off to the laundry room.

"So how did you deal with the monster this time?" Dad asked. "Was it anything like the hamsters? Did you use milk?"

"Gross," Martin muttered and then made a face. I guess we really WERE more alike than I thought.

"No. This time it was bright light."

"Neat!" Dad grinned.

"Yeah, I guess."

"Wait..."—Martin glanced over at me—"What did milk do to the hamsters?"

"It turned them back into normal hamsters," I said.

"Oh." Martin frowned.

"You okay, Martin?" I asked.

"Yeah," Martin said. "It's just... My dad had a thing for milk. And this whole thing with that trail has me thinking..."

Milton had been leaning closer trying to listen. He perked up at the mention of his dad. "Daddy? Milk? Daddy used to keep milk all around the house, even though me and Martin HATE IT!"

Oh my gosh, MORE MILK?!

"Your daddy just listened to too many of Grandpa Theo's silly stories is all," said Auntie Morgan. She started taking off Milton's coat and hat in an attempt to see just how dirty he'd gotten. "Milton, you're SOAKED! And where are your hearing aids?"

"Huh? Oh. The monster ate 'em!"

"Oh, Milton . . ." Her shoulders slumped. "Those are expensive."

"Mrs. Rose has one of them," I offered. I didn't want Milton to get into any more trouble.

"Well, that's something, I suppose," Auntie Morgan sighed. "Come on, baby boo, you're gettin' a bath before we take you home."

"What? A bath? Awwww!" Milton pouted. "At least let me take the cat with me! Kitty always needs a bath!"

I heard a rustling in the closet behind me. Mr. Fuzzikins slunk out and nuzzled my hand. "No, Mr. Fuzzikins," I whispered. "Be unseen!"

"Meow?"

"Kitty!" Milton cried out.

I picked up Mr. Fuzzikins and walked toward Milton. He was my little cousin, and I'd learned that he was a good kid. "Mr. Fuzzikins doesn't like baths, Milton."

"What?" I wasn't sure if Milton was confused or if he hadn't heard me.

"He likes to be petted." I leaned in with my fuzzy buddy in my arms. "GENTLY petted."

Milton looked irritated for a moment but then lightly stroked Mr. Fuzzikins's fur. Mr. Fuzzikins purred. Truly a paragon of virtue and forgiveness 'twas my kitty.

Oh my gosh, I'd almost forgotten! I grabbed my backpack and pulled out a still-wet Mr. Bear.

"Okay, stinky bears. Time for a bath!" Auntie Morgan and Milton disappeared upstairs.

Mom reappeared from the laundry room with a stack of rags and some of my clothes. "You can take turns in the shower after Milton's de-grunged." Mom pulled two chairs into the entry way. "Wipe off as much as you can and DON'T sit on the couch."

"Okay, Mom." I yawned and my stomach growled. Life-and-death struggle makes me tired and hungry, apparently.

Mom chuckled. "And then we can all have dinner." She and Dad went back to the kitchen. Dishes clattered and pots clanged as they got busy getting things ready.

Martin and I rubbed the worm gunk and mud off as best we could. The rain pattered the roof and rolled down the dark windows. Mr. Fuzzikins purred on my lap. He actually WAS going to need a bath after sitting on me.

Martin put his towel down. "Thank you, Teddy."

"For what?"

"You know for what." Martin clapped me on the shoulder. Ow. "If you hadn't been looking for things like the worm, there's no way I'd have been able to find Milton. He'd have gone missing just like my dad."

"Well... You know... You'd have done the same for me."

"Of course I would," said Martin. "But if someone had told me that my scaredy-cat cousin was chasing monsters, I'd have called them a liar!"

"It's not that simple," I grumbled.

"I guess you've changed a bit since I saw you last."

"Yeah, I guess." I squirmed. This kind of talk made me uncomfortable.

"Why did you want to go looking for stuff like that anyways?" Martin asked.

"I... Well..."

← He's not gonna understand, Teddy!

"Umm..."

He thinks that you're here to help, Teddy! He doesn't know that you wanna LEAVE him! →

"Teddy?"

← He doesn't know that you want to ABANDON him!

I CAN'T KEEP IT IN ANYMORE!

"No! I . . . I thought if I could prove to my parents that this place was dangerous, they might wanna move back to Kamloops."

"But Teddy, why—"

"I'm sorry, okay?! I'm sorry! This place is dangerous, and dark, and infested with evil things with too many teeth and it NEVER STOPS RAINING!"

"What? No, I was gonna—"

"And don't tell me it's not! After what happened tonight you CAN'T tell me this place isn't dangerous!"

"Really?" I asked. "You're not angry?"

"Of course not. Why would I be angry?"

"I . . . I didn't think you'd understand. I was afraid of what Tienna and Shane would say, too."

"If it makes you feel better, I won't tell them, Teddy. But if they're really your friends, they'll understand. I'm happy you're here. Really REALLY happy. I think this is the first time Mom's smiled in weeks. But I can totally understand why you'd want to move back to

Kamloops. I mean, I get homesick after a day or two away! I was gonna say something else, though."

"Oh."

"I was gonna ask, if you wanted proof, why didn't you just ask Heather to come over to your house with Biscuit? I mean, a talking evil hamster would convince anybody!"

About the Creator

© Samantha Foraie, 4A Photography Kamloops

Braden is certainly not a wormy alien monster and is much more likely a teacher, author, and illustrator. Braden lives in Kamloops, British Columbia (definitely not in the dimension just beyond the mists) and likes drawing oodles of doodles, writing stories that will still feature evil hamsters, playing lots and lots of role playing games like Dungeons & Dragons, and occasionally playing board games with his many nieces and nephews. His dream is to return home with interesting things from your dimension and . . . Sorry, scratch that last bit. His dream is to keep illustrating and writing. Yes. Illustrating and writing. That's all.

Secrets of Ravensbarrow, book 3 coming in Fall 2025!